JA-RAEL'S LIONESS

Angelique Anjou

Futuristic Romance

New Concepts   Georgia

Be sure to check out our website for the very best in fiction at fantastic prices!

When you visit our webpage, you can:

* Read excerpts of currently available books
* View cover art of upcoming books and current releases
* Find out more about the talented artists who capture the magic of the writer's imagination on the covers
* Order books from our backlist
* Find out the latest NCP and author news--including any upcoming book signings by your favorite NCP author
* Read author bios and reviews of our books
* Get NCP submission guidelines
* And so much more!

We also have contests and sales regularly, so be sure to visit our webpage to find the best deals in ebooks and paperbacks! To find out about our new releases as soon as they are available, please be sure to sign up for our newsletter (http://www.newconceptspublishing.com/newsletter.htm) or join our reader group (http://groups.yahoo.com/group/new_concepts_pub/join) !

The newsletter is available by double opt in only and our customer information is *never* shared!

Visit our webpage at:
www.newconceptspublishing.com

Ja-Rael's Lioness is an original publication of NCP. This work has never before appeared in book form. This work is a novel. Any similarity to actual persons or events is purely coincidental.

New Concepts Publishing
5202 Humphreys Rd.
Lake Park, GA 31636

ISBN 1-58608-697-9
© copyright 2005 Angelique Anjou
Cover art by Jenny Dixon, © copyright 2005

NCP books are available at special quantity discounts for bulk purchases for sales promotions, premiums, fund raising, or educational use. For details, write, email, or phone New Concepts Publishing, 5202Humphreys Rd., Lake Park, GA 31636, ncp@newconceptspublishing.com, Ph. 229-257-0367, Fax 229-219-1097.

First NCP Paperback Printing: 2005

Other Titles from NCP by Angelique Anjou:

Dream Warriors
Tears of the Dragon (Now available in Trade Paperback)

Chapter One

Like everyone else, Elise was grateful to be alive, grateful the computer had found a habitable planet to set down on. She had probably reminded herself of that fact every single day over the past two years since their ship had negotiated a landing on the planet of Tor, now arbitrarily renamed New Earth by the interlopers, of which she was one.

It wasn't Earth. It was close enough to sustain dispossessed Earthlings, but it still missed the mark by a long shot--at least, old Earth, in the days before their home world had entered its death throes and begun to try to annihilate the parasites poisoning it.

She remembered. The golden age had been before her time, when civilization had reached a technological peak that guaranteed comfort for perhaps half the world's inhabitants. The economy and the ecology of the world had been reasonably stable then, according to what she'd learned in school, but even when the golden age had begun its decline and decay, the Earth hadn't been half bad. There were a lot of days when one could see beautiful blue skies, plenty of days when it felt good just to go outside. There'd been enough food, enough water, luxuries that could still be bought. There'd been leisure time. There'd been entertainment and time to enjoy it.

Earth had become wildly unstable long before the meteor hit it, however. Like everyone else, she'd clung to life by the skin of her teeth, just trying to survive while nature wreaked havoc, destroying pretty much everything man had built.

Tor was stable, but it wasn't like Earth in any period that she knew of, or had even read about. The gravity was roughly the same, the size, the components that made up the atmosphere, but it was closer to its sun than Earth had been ... which meant that it was hot in the winter, and hotter in the summer.

Within the first week of landing on Tor, pretty much everyone had disposed of most of their clothing. They had brought all of the technology they could cram into their ship, and all the knowledge, and all the supplies, but it still took human labor to build, to hunt and grow food, and that meant exposure to the heat and humidity of Tor--New Earth.

Elise couldn't help but think it ironic that they'd traveled light-years only to find a world that was just about as fucking miserable as the one they'd left.

She shook the thought off. "I'm grateful to be alive," she muttered, wondering where the other evacuees had ended up.

They'd left Earth like viral spores, climbed aboard ship with no destination in mind, programmed their computers to find a place to live and scurried into their hyber units. A dozen different ships could have landed on Tor and they might never know it. They'd become 'cave' people, primitives, eking out an existence on a world not their own.

They were lucky the Torrines tolerated them, especially since, like children fearful of the dark, they'd established their colony within spitting distance of one of the larger Torrine cities. Because, despite the fact that the Torrines didn't make any bones about the fact that they weren't thrilled to have them, it gave the Earthlings comfort to be near civilization, even if it wasn't theirs.

Spying a fallen log and the 'shrooms' they'd discovered were not only edible, but pretty damned good, Elise dismissed her internal complaining, feeling a surge of relief as she moved quickly to the log and knelt to pick them. It looked like enough to fill her basket. Once she'd gathered her quota, she could retreat to the habitat and cool off.

There were poison shrooms among them, but she knew the difference. Not that it mattered, really, except that grabbing the wrong thing would mean she hadn't filled her quota and she'd have to go looking again. They never ate anything until they'd run it through the analyzer and checked it carefully, so she didn't have to worry about making everyone sick--or worse.

Lord help them if the thing ever malfunctioned, or just wore out!

It was beginning to look like technology, for them, was going to become a thing of the past, though. Unlike some of the ships, theirs hadn't boasted the most desirable balance of necessaries. They had three doctors (all specialists who knew virtually nothing beyond their field), but no nurses, a half a dozen engineers, but only one electronic repair technician, mechanics--but few things in need of mechanics, growers, but very little farming tools, equipment, or even plants or seeds. She was a teacher, one of a dozen, and there were only two children above the age of infancy, and one of them, the nineteen year old, couldn't actually be classified as a child.

She should've known she was in the wrong line. She was always in the wrong damned line!

Or maybe not. Maybe it had been preordained that she end up just where she had just by being who and what she was, a world class procrastinator and terminal optimist.

Their ship could have been named the *USS Misfit*, the *USS Leftovers*. Or maybe the *USS Dumbshits Who Thought it Would All Blow Over and They Wouldn't Have to Leave*.

Elise paused in her task, arching her aching back and rubbing it. It occurred to her after a moment that her foul mood wasn't just the heat. She was dog tired and hungry to boot. No wonder she had opticalrectumitis!

She studied the shrooms speculatively, but as hungry as she was, she didn't quite dare try them raw. It was one thing to have a good opinion of one's knowledge and something else entirely to stake one's life on it.

* * * *

In general, Ja-rael didn't especially look forward to the annual trade fair on Tor. Unlike his own world, Meeri, the weather on Tor was miserable and he was generally so worn out from the heat and humidity by the second day of trading that all he really wanted to do was unload his beasts, take whatever he could, and head home. This time, however, he was on a mission.

This time he intended to come away with something he could use to barter for a mate.

He *had* to do something or the fire in his blood was going to eat a hole in his brain and leave him dangerously, savagely insane.

He'd known when he had decided to become a healer that he would never be a rich man. The way of the physician was only taught to those who were willing to dedicate themselves to helping any in need and that meant settling for what they could afford to pay. He did not regret it. He had never regretted his choice, but there were very few who could afford to pay much for his help, and many who could afford nothing at all. He had been forced by his own needs to supplement his livelihood by spending much of his time trapping the narlo for trade with the Torrine, who valued the beast far more than the Meeri.

He'd been appalled when he had finally woken to the fact that he was halfway through his prime breeding years and still had not taken a mate. Every year that passed reduced his chance of producing any female offspring at all and if he were not careful he would find himself beyond his prime altogether, and he might not even have a male child.

Of course, there were always exceptions. He knew of several males who had mated late and still managed to produce offspring--male, of course, no females--but they were fortunate even in that. The females were hard to convince to produce at all, and they completely lost interest in their mate once he passed his prime years when he would produce the strongest, healthiest of offspring.

He had never liked to trust to fate, however. The odds were against him that he would be one of those rare individuals who managed to produce a late cub. Beyond that, he was sick to death of his own company, and even sicker of the company of the other single males, who did very little beyond complain about the cost of acquiring a mate and the lack of interest the females displayed in them even when they managed to get one.

These days females were so scarce and hard to come by that a male had to be rich even to catch a glimpse of one. The worst of it was that any male fortunate enough to produce more than two female offspring was usually so well set up already that it was hard to tempt them to part with a daughter. They knew damned well that no matter how much one suitor might offer, the next would offer more, and the one after that even more. So long as they didn't hold out too long, until the female was beyond her reproductive years, they could pretty well name their price.

He was a healer, not a scientist, but it didn't take a scientist to figure out that it was the Meeri mating practices that were almost entirely responsible for the fact that there were fewer females with every generation--fewer offspring at all, for that matter. Regardless of whether the male was a prime producer or not, he was lucky to land a mate able to produce two before she ceased producing at all, and in their latter years the females were even less interested in producing than the young females were.

It made things pretty miserable for the male. The *only* time a Meeri female was willing to mate at all was if there was a chance for breeding a cub. If she'd already produced two healthy cubs, she rarely wanted a third and if her mate was beyond prime breeding years, it didn't matter whether she'd even had one or not, she just plain couldn't be convinced.

It was the bane of every Meeri male's existence that males desperately wanted intercourse with their mate purely for the enjoyment of the act itself, whether there was any chance of producing at all.

The misery of such a life should have been enough to convince the single males to remain single, but desperation was the key word in the equation. A taste of the pie was better than none of it, and as well guarded as the females were, there wasn't a chance in hell of getting hold of a female *without* mating. The law stated that any male who did was to be castrated, but that was one law that hadn't been tested in his memory. The unwritten law was death and the family of the stolen female didn't even have to take care of that themselves. The outraged males who had been trying to barter for her generally settled the matter.

Naturally enough, stealing a mate was a rare occurrence on Meeri, but he had no trouble understanding what drove those who'd tried it.

Desperation.

It was hard to accept the fact that you were never going to have a mate at all because you couldn't accumulate enough wealth to barter for one no matter how hard you worked.

That wasn't going to be a problem for him, however. There was only one time of the year that the worlds of Meeri and Tor were close enough to allow for trading, but that had given him all the time he needed to round up his bartering goods. He was damned good at trapping. He had two dozen narlo in the hold of his ship. The Torrines were going to be falling over themselves to trade for such a highly prized delicacy, but he was armed to the teeth and he wasn't letting a single one go for less than three zihnars--which was almost as prized on Meeri as the narlo was on Tor, and he was pretty damned sure that he could barter for a mate with three dozen zihnars! Hell, he could probably even get a *choice* mate for that many zihnars!

Chapter Two

Elise had been walking for some time along the path before she became aware enough of her surroundings to wonder where she was. She stopped, thinking at first that it was just the sort of disorientation generally associated with daydreaming. She'd expected to see something else and that was why nothing looked familiar. After carefully studying her entire surroundings, however, she realized that it wasn't just momentary disorientation. She was in a part of the jungle she'd never been in before.

Above the tops of the trees to the east, she could see the spires of the Torrine city. She'd only visited the city a few times since they'd arrived. The Torrines were a people who enjoyed trade, but the colonists had discovered quickly enough that the Torrines had very little interest in anything they had to trade. Moreover, theirs was an extremely male dominated society. The females rarely went out in public at all, and never without being draped from head to toe in veils and the escort of an armed male guard.

Fortunately, they appeared to have absolutely no interest in the Earth females, but that didn't stop them from being extremely disapproving of the customs practiced by the Earth people. Consequently, as much as the colonists would've liked to intermingle with the only other civilized species on the planet, except for trading whenever they could for whatever they happened to need, everyone pretty much kept to themselves.

She'd been so involved in her internal bitching she'd taken a wrong turn, heading east when she should've been heading west.

Sighing, Elise glanced down at her shrooms. They were already beginning to look limp from the heat. If she didn't hurry, everyone was going to be complaining about her coming back with wilted food hardly fit to eat.

Getting her bearings, she turned back the way she'd just come and quickened her step, trying to make up for the time she'd lost wandering around the jungle.

* * * *

Ja-rael's landing was more of a controlled crash that a smooth landing, but then he wasn't much of a pilot and the crate he was flying wasn't much of a ship. It hadn't been when he'd traded for it. In fact, it hadn't been operational when he'd traded for it. He'd had the devil of a time finding anyone who knew enough about the thing to get it going and an even harder time finding someone to teach him how to fly it after he'd gotten it fixed.

Mentally, he shrugged. As long as it got him back to Meeri this time, he didn't care if it ever flew again. One way or another, this was his last trip. Either he would get enough to get himself a mate--or he wouldn't. Every moment he dedicated to his own personal gain was time he deprived his patients of medical attention they might need desperately. He couldn't allow himself to become so self-absorbed as to ignore the needs of those who trusted him with their health, and often their lives.

The narlo, he discovered, had made the trip well enough, but, despite the herbs he'd fed them to keep them calm, they were quaking with fear and thirsty besides since they'd become so panicked they'd turned over the trough of water he'd left for them.

Sighing, he grabbed a bucket. There was a stream near the landing field on the outskirts of Miazina. It was going to be a long haul for carrying water, but he was pretty sure his piloting skills weren't sufficient to move the ship any closer to the source. Besides, the narlo needed time to calm down before he could herd them into Miazina.

Leaving the ship, he glanced up at the sky to get his bearings and then struck off through the jungle in a more or less straight shot toward the stream. It would've been easier to take the well worn path, but it would take a lot longer, too, since the path wandered in first one direction and then another. He was sweating from the heat and humidity by the time he reached the stream. Setting the bucket on the bank, Ja-rael dove in to cool off before he headed back.

He'd just emerged when he saw something that sent a shock wave through him, that so stunned him that he might well have drowned if not for the fact that he had his feet planted firmly on the bed of the stream.

Many moments passed before his stunned mind could even begin to assimilate what it was that he was looking at, and even then he was more inclined to think he was hallucinating, for, despite the legends, he'd never believed such a creature actually existed, or ever had for that matter.

It was a maned lioness.

Torn between the fear that his mind had snapped, absolute fascination, disbelief, and the anxiety that any movement would make the vision vanish, he remained frozen to the spot, trying to jog his mind into functioning.

He didn't know whether to be more horrified or thrilled when she stopped and knelt beside the stream to drink and bathe.

She was the most beautiful creature he'd ever beheld in his entire life. It took his breath away, just looking at her. Her mane--streaked with gold and red--framed her lovely face, flowing from just above her brow, across the crown of her head, and then hanging loosely almost to her rounded hips, fascinating him as the wind and her movements lifted it, made it float and flutter around her like the finest of veils.

She wore nothing else beyond her mane and the short veil tied at one hip.

He realized he hadn't even dared to breathe just about the time she pulled the veil off and his gaze fastened on the tiny triangle shaped pelt between her legs that matched the mane on her head almost perfectly in color.

He sucked in a breath of wonder then. His cock, too stunned to react before, and chilled by the water besides, stood up abruptly.

Almost as if she smelled his desire, she froze, lifting her head cautiously and glancing around.

Ja-rael held the breath he'd just sucked in, feeling every muscle in his body tense.

His mind glazed, however. Every rational thought fled.

She was alone.

There wasn't a single male in sight.

And she was a legendary maned lioness--his for taking.

His mouth went dry, but neither doubt nor fear entered his mind. He had to have her. If he died in the attempt, so be it.

* * * *

The urge to stop at the stream for a drink of water and to cool off was just too tempting to pass up. Elise knelt, setting her basket on the ground beside her, and scooped up several handfuls of water to soothe her parched throat. When she'd drank her fill, she splashed the water up her arms and over her face and neck. A little shiver traveled through her as the cold water cascaded over her heated skin. It felt good, though, so good she wanted to just jump in and let the cool water wash the sticky heat from her all over.

She'd already untied her sarong when a strange sensation washed over her, like a flash of heat, almost like ants crawling over her skin, making the fine hairs on her body prickle. Directly behind that, she felt a barely discernible wave of dizziness and then she detected a faint, completely unidentifiable scent. Lifting her head, she sniffed curiously. She realized then that it wasn't something she smelled. It was internal, a chemical reaction within her body, rather like when the metallic taste of blood floods one's senses, except this was pleasant.

It was more than pleasant. It was intoxicating. The heat that flooded through her was as internal as the chemical she'd thought she had smelled. Her body quickened. Blood rushed into even the tiniest of vessels. This time, however, it didn't feel like ants swarming over her. It was as stimulating as a touch, making her heart struggle harder, making it difficult to draw a deep breath into her lungs.

She was so focused upon that internal quickening she might not have even noticed the creature that rose from the water and moved purposefully toward her, except that the moment he emerged, the sensations increased tenfold. Like the concussion of an exploding bomb, it moved over her in a wave, draining the strength from her.

He caught her to him as if he more than half suspected that she would try to run, but running was the furthest thing from her mind. She wanted him to touch her, needed it, needed a lot more than that.

Scooping her into his arms, he began to jog rapidly through the jungle.

Elise was only vaguely aware of it. She'd looped her arms around his neck when he hoisted her against his chest.

She stroked a curious hand over him, fascinated with the silky feel of his flesh. Dimly, she realized it wasn't skin like her own, but skin covered in an almost microscopic fuzz--like peach fuzz, her mind supplied. He glanced at her almost curiously as she ran a hand over his head.

She liked his eyes. They were beautiful, golden, cat-like.

She liked his smell.

She loved the way he felt, his body taut, his flesh silky against her palm and her fingers.

His ears were interesting, too. They lay flat against the sides of his head, but instead of a rounded shell as her ears were, his came to a very definite point. She traced the swirls of his ears.

A shudder went through him that delighted her.

She tightened her arms, moving close enough to nuzzle his neck and then his ear. "Make love to me," she murmured.

He made a strangled sound in his throat that was almost like a growl and moved faster until he was almost running.

The jogging gait made it impossible for Elise to examine him as she would've liked, but then it occurred to her that he must be looking for a place to make love to her. Impatience moved through her.

She really didn't want to wait. She was so hot now, she felt as if she was going to come without him if he didn't hurry and she didn't want that.

Relief flooded her when they emerged from the jungle and she saw a wreck of a space craft sitting in a clearing. He raced toward it and up the gang plank, setting her on her feet at last.

She curled around him as he worked the lever to raise the gang plank, stroking his arms, his back, reaching down in search of his member.

Delightful heat flashed through her, making her belly clench as her fingers closed around this turgid flesh. He stiffened, pushed her roughly against one wall.

Elise groaned, rubbing her mound against his hard thigh, wishing she was just a little taller so that she could envelop his hard cock in her cleft.

Chapter Three

Some primal instinct guided Ja-rael, for he had long since lost the ability for rational thought. His brain was wrapped in a heated, red haze that prevented any sort of recognizable thought pattern. Despite that, he was aware of a trace of both surprise and confusion.

The female should have screamed. She should have fought him tooth and nail when he grabbed her and hauled her off.

Instead, she caressed him, examining him with a curiosity and desire that seemed equal to his own and only further decimated his ability to think.

He had no idea how he found his way back to his ship. He hadn't been able to focus on anything beyond the warm body he clutched so desperately-- and her touch. He was reluctant even to release her long enough to retract the gang plank and close the hatch, fearful she would come to her senses and flee, but he couldn't hold her and manage it, and he was just as fearful that, by now, a pride of males were in hot pursuit and would wrest her from him before he could make his getaway.

The moment he released her, however, she curled around him, rubbing her body against him in a way that almost made him spill his seed when he hadn't even entered her yet. Frantically, he worked the levers to lock the ship down. The moment he heard the grinding whir that signaled the closing of the hatch, he grabbed her and shoved her against the bulkhead.

He couldn't think beyond mating--that very instant. If he hadn't feared pursuit, he would've thrown her down on the grass and mated with her before they ever reached the ship.

As it was, he was in no condition to consider the undesirability of trying to mate with her standing. He knew the mechanics of mating, of course, but naturally enough he'd never actually done so or he might have realized that he would regret not seeking a soft pallet to lie upon.

She wrapped her arms around him, hoisted herself up his body and then wrapped her legs around his waist, however, and the instant she did, he grabbed his cock and began struggling to force it inside her.

* * * *

Elise thought she was going to die if he didn't get his cock inside of her. Her heart was pounding so hard it felt like it would rupture at any moment and she'd gasped for breath until she was holding onto consciousness by a thread. Almost the instant she felt his cock spreading her, entering her, her body began to quake with release. She groaned, squeezing her eyes closed as it ripped through her. The convulsions of her release only made it that much harder for him to claim her fully. By the time he'd managed to sink deeply inside of her, she'd climaxed again and felt herself climbing upward toward a third.

She *was* going to die, she thought as he began pounding into her with a desperation that matched hers.

She clung to him tightly, riding the wave upward once more. This time when it caught her the rapture was so explosive she screamed with the hard jolts that wracked her body.

He growled, low in his throat and his body began to convulse as he found his own release.

Elise hung limply against him, gasping for breath, barely conscious.

Abruptly, the cock inside of her, instead of deflating, seemed almost to double in size, pressing outward against the walls of her sex uncomfortably. The sensation brought Elise back from the edge of consciousness. "What the hell is that?"

The man--male whateverthehellhewas that was holding her was still gasping for breath. He lifted his head weakly and stared at her blankly.

Belatedly, Elise realized that there was probably about a one in a trillion chance that he would understand English.

He wasn't Torrine--she didn't think, unless there were other races she hadn't seen. She cast about in her mind for the little she knew of the Torrine language, however, figuring he wouldn't be here, near the Torrine city, unless he'd come to trade, which meant he would have to have some grasp of the language.

"Get that damned thing out of me," she growled.

He blinked at her stupidly.

Maybe he didn't understand Torrine after all?

Elise tried to push him away, tried to get her feet on the deck below her. His arms tightened, pinning her in place.

"You know I can't," he said through gritted teeth, more as if he was in pain, however, than as a response to her own furious demand.

"What do you mean you can't?"

He gave her a curious look. "I've spilled my seed inside of you. My phallus has sealed the cavity to prevent the loss of my seed."

Fury washed through Elise then. "Jesus fucking Christ!" she growled angrily. "Are you saying you've impregnated me?"

He blinked. "We mated," he said a little weakly, obviously thoroughly confused by her attitude.

"Let me go. NOW!"

Her anger finally stirred his. "I can *not*," he growled, demonstrating the truth by tugging a couple of times.

Oh god! They were fucking stuck! "This can't be happening," Elise muttered. "It's a nightmare. Any minute I'm going to wake up. I must have eaten one of those damned shrooms."

She fumed for a few moments. She could tell the guy was beginning to suffer from the strain of holding them both upright in such an awkward position, however, and his suffering mollified her a little.

When she glanced at him again, she saw that he was studying her, not surprisingly, as if he'd never seen anything like her.

She hadn't seen anything like him either.

He looked almost human--except for the stripes, the cat eyes, the pointed ears, the fuzz covered flesh and--let us not forget-- the post coital expanding cock!

In a dark alley, she mentally amended, she might have mistaken him for a human--or if she'd been wearing a blindfold. Except for the fuzz, he didn't have a hair on him, though. She couldn't exactly call him bald--his head was covered with the same fine down as the rest of his body-- but it didn't look as if it grew like human hair--as if it had been cut, or shaved close to his head. His features, except for those cat eyes and the pointed ears, looked very human.

Actually, as much as she hated to admit it, he was really a very handsome alien being. She couldn't think of a single human male in the colony that was even half as easy on the eyes. She didn't know what it was that made her think so. His features were regular and well proportioned, like his body, appealingly shaped, but taken individually not especially lovely. Taken as a whole, his features formed a very nice face, though.

Now that the heat was gone, and his eyes weren't glazed with ecstasy, she noticed there was intelligence in his eyes, as well.

"Why did you grab me?" she asked almost mildly.

His gaze flickered to her face. "You were unguarded. I ... couldn't resist."

Unguarded. Maybe he was one of the Torrine races? That sounded as if his customs were very much the same, anyway.

"You can't just ... steal me away!" she said indignantly.

His jaw set, but she could see that he was embarrassed by his impulsiveness. She didn't know how she knew, but she did.

"I can pay," he ground out.

If he'd slapped her she wouldn't have been any more insulted. "Pay!"

"I have the mate price."

Elise stared at him blankly for several moments. "What are you talking about?"

He looked uncomfortable. "I brought trade goods to barter for a mate. I can pay your sire."

These people *bought* their brides? "You don't have enough money to buy me," she growled threateningly.

His eyes narrowed. "That is for your sire to decide," he retorted arrogantly.

Chapter Four

It was a hell of a conversation to be having while they were stuck together like Siamese twins--sort of. She supposed, however, that discussing the weather wouldn't have made it any better.

The thought had scarcely occurred to her when, to her immense relief, she felt a loosening inside of her.

He looked as relieved as she felt, pulling away from her and allowing her to slide to the deck as he adjusted the loincloth he wore.

Elise had to lock her knees to keep from sliding right on down to the floor.

She studied him warily while she watched him adjust his clothing, what little there was.

She didn't even have that much. Dimly, she recalled taking her sarong off to bathe in the river--and not a hell of a lot after that. The only thing that was really clear in her mind was an absolute desperation to scratch the itch that was driving her out of her mind. What had he done to her, she wondered?

She knew it had to have been him.

She thought it must have been.

Maybe it *was* the shrooms? But she couldn't remember eating any of them. For that matter, she couldn't remember anything in the chemical readouts that would indicate the presence of such a drug.

It was one hell of a drug, though. She'd been on fire. She had *never* felt anything like that before in her life, not even close. This went way beyond desire. It was the aphrodisiac to end all--in more ways than one. She'd thought she was going to die if she couldn't mount his cock, and quickly. Dimly, and with a good deal of embarrassment, she recalled clawing and scratching at him when he didn't move fast enough to suit her.

Small wonder he'd looked so confused afterwards when she'd snarled at him.

And she'd climaxed three times, so hard she'd thought she would die from it.

A shiver chased its way through her at the memory and she shied away from it. "I don't have a sire," she said tartly. "At least--I suppose I do, but I have no idea of where he is. Anyway, *we* don't do this sort of thing."

She saw that he was frowning.

"Who is your male protector?"

Boy oh boy did he have a one track mind. "Look. Just take me back and we'll forget this happened, ok?"

He looked at her like she'd lost her mind. "No."

Elise blinked. "What do you mean, no?"

"No. I have chosen you for my mate. I risked ... all to have you. I will pay the mate price, but I will not give you back."

"Look, Tarzan! I'm not interested in having a damned mate--especially not one that isn't even the same species. I want to get back to my own people!"

He looked both angry and confused by that, but he focused on the mating thing again. "We *did* mate. You seemed willing enough."

Elise blushed to the roots of her hair. That was putting it nicely. She'd been all over him, trying to grab his cock and mount it without his help. She could tell, though, that he wasn't much more clear on what had happened between them than she was. Most likely that accounted for his diplomacy--the fact that he wasn't entirely certain she hadn't been trying to fight him off. "Well, I don't know what came over me, but that was ... it must have been the shrooms. I think I ate something that made me act strange-- not myself-- but I'm fine now and I want to go home!"

"Home is with me now."

Elise's eyes narrowed. "I'm trying to be civil about this, Tarzan, but enough is enough. I'm not going anywhere with you. I sure as hell am not going off to god knows where to play Jane and live in your tree house."

He frowned. "My name is Ja-rael, not Tarzan, and I do not live in the trees. I live on Meeri and I have a domicile in the city of Mordun."

"What's Meeri?" Elise asked curiously, distracted by the strange name.

"The sister world of Tor."

There was a sister world?

She was standing in a space craft for god's sake! Why was it that it hadn't occurred to her that this was a member of an intelligent, advanced civilization?

Because he looked as if his race had evolved from cat like creatures and therefore he couldn't *possibly* be as superior as a human? "So--you're not from here?"

"No."

"Ok, well neither am I, and I think there's just been a little misunderstanding here. I'm from Earth, see, another world a long, long, long way from here, and I'm human, not Torrine."

A confused frown drew his brows together. He studied her for several moments, his expression changing from confusion to fascination. "You are a maned lioness--so beautiful you take my breath," he said as he caught a strand of her hair between his fingertips and rubbed it experimentally. "I will cherish you as you deserve, give all that is within my power to provide for you and our young. I am only a healer, but I am a good trapper. I will do well for you. I give you my word."

Elise would've continued arguing except for the fact that that odd sense of strangeness had begun to creep over her again--flashes of heat, dizziness.

"I have never seen such exquisite, delicate markings on any female," he murmured, tracing the freckles sprinkled across her cheeks and nose.

Elise closed her eyes, trying to fight off the waves of heat curling inside of her, building until she could scarcely catch her breath. It was useless. Closing her eyes only seemed to make the sensations intensify more rapidly until she felt herself reeling out of control, found that she couldn't contain the urge to touch him back. In truth, she wasn't aware of touching him until she felt the silkiness of his flesh beneath her palms and the hard strength of his muscles beneath that. She moved closer, stroking her body along his.

A look that was a mixture of desire, confusion, and desperation crossed his features. Abruptly, he scooped her up and headed down the corridor with her. Elise found it very unsatisfactory. She'd been enjoying rubbing her body all over his. Now all she could reach was his shoulders and neck.

She contented herself with nuzzling his neck and nipping at his ear with her teeth.

He shuddered and moved faster.

They fell together onto a soft pallet, but Elise was beyond caring if they'd landed on the deck. She felt almost sick with desperation. Her sex was throbbing painfully for his possession. If possible, it was even worse than before, as if, now that she'd experienced it, her body had already begun craving him. "Now, Ja-rael! Now!"

He stroked her, almost soothingly. "I want to love you, Jane."

"Now!" she virtually snarled, groping blindly for his cock for several moments before she managed to grasp it.

He flinched, but he allowed her to guide it home, thrusting into her.

She groaned, shuddering as he entered her and she felt her body begin to quake almost at once in culmination. By the time he'd attained his rhythm, her body was already escalating toward another, harder peak. She stroked the flexing muscles of his arms and back, nuzzled his neck. Blindly, she sought his lips, brushing hers across them.

He gasped, jerking in surprise when she fitted her mouth against his, sucking at first his upper lip and then the lower one. When he gasped, she slipped her tongue into his mouth, feeling a fiery rush as his taste and scent washed into her. Groaning, he mimicked her movements, tasting her mouth in turn.

The kiss sent them both over the edge into an explosion of ecstasy.

Elise collapsed weakly beneath him, skating the edge of consciousness. Without a whimper of protest, she gave it up, drifting away on the cloud of bliss he'd created.

Ja-rael lifted slightly away from her and studied her for several moments in consternation before he realized that she slept. Relief flooded him, partly because he'd worried that he'd hurt her and partly because he had a sneaking suspicion she wouldn't have been any happier about their mating this time than she had been before.

Propping on one elbow, he studied her in the dim light in his cabin and finally lifted his other hand, stroking her satiny skin, marveling over the texture of it and the tiny markings that sprinkled her skin.

He could scarcely believe his good fortune. He had thought only of acquiring a mate, had known that he would have to settle for whatever female he could barter for. In the back of his mind, he'd known she would most likely not even be pretty, let alone beautiful, and probably nearing the end of her breeding years.

He would have to guard his Jane assiduously. Ordinarily, the males stayed clear of the females that had already been claimed and mated, but Jane was so lovely a male could be expected to loose his head.

Look at what he'd done, and he was ordinarily very level headed.

He frowned after a moment, trying to recall, and make sense of, the conversation they'd had before. She spoke Torrine--and not at all well. The language she'd used before had been completely incomprehensible, though.

Why did she not speak one of the dialects of Meeri? Or Tor for that matter, since it appeared that she lived here?

He wracked his brain, trying to remember the details of the legends of the maned race, but, in truth, he'd never had much interest in what he'd thought were merely stories to entertain children. He gave up on it after only a few moments. He was far more disturbed that she didn't seem willing to accept the mating.

It was done. Why would she regret it? She could have refused. Even in the state he'd been in at the time, he would not have been able to mate her if she'd refused. Regardless of his reprehensible behavior, he was not a beast.

For that matter, he couldn't figure out why she refused to accept him one moment and the next demanded that he mate her again.

She *had* demanded it. If he hadn't been the next thing to mindless at the time himself, he might have been alarmed by the aggressiveness of her behavior.

He felt the first stirrings of arousal at that thought and immediately turned his thoughts elsewhere. If he became aroused again, her people were likely to find him here when they came to search for her.

It was all very well to think of dying of bliss, but he had no desire to be killed while in the throes of passion, no desire to die at all.

That thought was enough to cool his ardor and when at last his phallus slipped from her body, he eased off the pallet quietly and left the cabin, locking it behind him.

He had to think and he couldn't think straight when he was near her.

Settling in the pilot's seat, he stretched his long legs out and propped them on the console, staring out at the field as dusk settled over it.

There was no sign of searchers.

But maybe they were hiding in the jungle, waiting to see if he was foolhardy enough to come out?

Mentally, he shrugged. Foolhardy or not, he was going to have to. He'd been so caught up in making off with Jane he'd forgotten all about the water for the narlo.

Sitting up decisively, he grabbed his weapon and strode down the corridor to the hatch. Seeing no movement in the trees, he opened it and went out.

Chapter Five

The bucket was where he'd left it. He made three trips from the stream to the ship, until he was satisfied his cargo of narlo was well supplied with water. When he checked on Jane, he saw that she was still sleeping.

Relieved, he returned to his seat in the cockpit to assess his predicament.

He still couldn't quite figure out what the situation was from what she'd told him. She'd said she had no sire, and had named no protector. She couldn't already have been claimed or she wouldn't have allowed him to mate with her.

Unless her mate had died?

If that was the case, though, there would have been a battle to claim her. She wouldn't simply have been abandoned to her own devices. Occasionally, a particularly unpleasant, older female, might go unclaimed, but in general there were so many males desperate for any female they could get that even the most vicious, ugliest female had her choice.

Maybe it was different here on Torrine? Maybe her tribe was so small that there were plenty of females to go around and the males didn't fight over them like they did on Meeri?

In a way, it made sense. The maned tribes had vanished from Meeri altogether, had sunk into mere legend. Perhaps a small group had managed to make it here in ancient times, when the races of Meeri had divided? The Torrine were the dominant race of Tor, however, and although they were willing enough to trade with the Meeri, there had never been any intermingling of the two races.

It was forbidden by Tor law, and the Meeri considered with contempt.

For their part, the Meeri simply found the Tor unappealing. Moreover, the Tor were just a little too fanatical in their customs to suit the Meeri folk. If the maned race had settled here and had not flourished--

perhaps because of the miserable heat--then they could well have dwindled to no more than a handful in this time for they would certainly not have had the opportunity to mingle with the Tor even if they'd wanted to.

Thinking about the Torrines and their customs sparked a memory of their earlier conversation and he puzzled over it.

She'd been outraged when he'd talked about offering a mating price for her. She'd been insulted. There was no doubt in his mind about that. He had some trouble understanding the Torrine she spoke, but none at all understanding the emotions that flashed across her face.

He could understand that her customs might be a good bit different than his, but to be insulted seemed extreme. What was wrong with offering compensation to the family that was losing a daughter? And it was more than that. It was proof that the male was a good provider and the daughter would live well. If he had been a sire giving up a daughter, he would certainly want to know that the male taking her would be taking very good care of her.

That thought led to his mating with Jane and he found his body reacting accordingly, which brought him to another thing that puzzled him.

The Meeri females seemed completely indifferent about mating. They were willing to do their duty and produce offspring, but it went no further than that. He was a healer. He'd had far more opportunity to observe this first hand than most Meeri males. He had not met a single one that embraced the situation with any enthusiasm, and it was only the most good-natured of females that allowed their mate occasional access to her charms if she'd already performed her duty.

And yet Jane seemed wildly enthusiastic, to say the least. It hadn't been because she wanted to produce, either. He was certain he hadn't misunderstood her outrage at that suggestion.

He couldn't imagine what she'd meant by saying they weren't the same species--a different race, yes, but obviously very closely related--the comment had made it clear, though, that she was not ready to breed offspring.

He discovered he could not coolly consider that aspect. The moment his mind thought 'breeding', his body jumped to the ready and visions of Jane writhing beneath him, stroking him, surfaced, arousing him even more.

He didn't know what that thing with the mouth had been about--a very strange custom indeed, *tasting* one's mate-- but it had felt almost as good as sliding through her hot, wet passage.

He dragged in a shuddering breath, trying to cool his heated arousal.

A low moan from the vicinity of his cabin didn't help matters at all and he finally got up and left the ship again.

After pacing the field near the ship for some time, Ja-rael realized that he needed

to see if he could ascertain just how much trouble he was in for stealing Jane before it landed squarely on top of him.

Ordinarily, it just was not done that a male stole his mate and then paid, but this was generally because a male didn't *get* desperate enough to steal his mate except when he *couldn't* pay. If they would just give him the chance, he would prove that he could and then he could take Jane and leave with an easy mind.

Of course, he could anyway. The two worlds were already beginning to move apart again. In a few days they would be out of range of any ship from Tor--until next year, of course, and by then it would be far too late. He would have a cub off of Jane and her family couldn't take her back. They'd have to settle for whatever he could pay.

Or, they could kill him and take her back just to prove a point.

He didn't really want to have that hanging over his head, though. He wanted to enjoy his mate. Once everything was settled, he knew Jane would cease demanding to be taken back.

Full darkness had descended by the time he made up his mind, but Ja-rael knew Jane's delicate fragrance as well as he knew his own by now. He had very little trouble following her path.

By the time the tiny orb that was Tor's moon rose to light his way, Ja-rael had been wandering through the jungle for more than an hour and he was more puzzled than ever. There didn't seem to be any rhyme or reason to her path. It simply wandered round and round through the jungle, crossing and re-crossing. He was on the verge of giving up and returning to the ship when he found a new path. This one seemed far more purposeful and he discovered when he'd followed it that it led to a large clearing.

In the center of the clearing was the strangest domicile he'd ever seen. It was rounded, like a hill. In fact, from what he could see, it looked like it had been constructed from soil. There were windows, however, here and there, and light spilled from them.

There wasn't a sign of any sort of patrols beyond the domicile.

There certainly wasn't any sign of searchers.

He didn't know what to make of that. It occurred to him after a few moments, though, that maybe Jane's tribe couldn't see well at night. He couldn't help but notice her pupils were strange. He hadn't dwelt on the defect--that one little flaw in an otherwise perfect creature only made her more endearing to him--but what if it was a tribal trait? Such a trait would almost certainly affect their night vision.

After several moments indecision, he decided to move closer for a better look. He'd been stomping through the clearing for some time before he realized it wasn't a clearing at all. It was a garden, and probably the most pathetic garden he'd ever seen.

He knelt, examining the plants.

They didn't look like anything he was familiar with, but it was pretty obvious from their stunted growth and limpness that the plants either didn't grow well in this area or the tribe had no growing skills.

Dismissing the puzzle for the moment, he moved more carefully toward the domicile. When he'd reached it, he began to circle it, glancing inside each time he came upon a window that was lit. Shock went through him at the very first window. It was Jane's tribe all right. He could tell by the manes, but there was one male and two females in the room. It took him several moments to figure that out because the three were entwined.

Outrage filled him when he realized that they were mating--all three of them.

The male had *two* females? Two! It was the most grossly unjust thing imaginable, to think that they had enough females that a male could have two!

They couldn't possibly appreciate them as they should if they had such an abundance. Maybe that was why no search parties had come for Jane?

His poor, darling mate! To think that she was such a beautiful creature and not even properly appreciated! They'd allowed her to wander off--alone--into the jungle and hadn't even come to look for her when she'd gone missing!

He was so angry that it was many moments before he actually began to notice what was proceeding in the room. He'd been watching for many minutes before it occurred to him that they were tasting each other--all over. Intrigued in spite of his outrage, he moved a little closer.

The man began to suckle the women's breasts. Ja-rael was repulsed at first, wondering if the males continued to suckle into adulthood, but then he noticed that the females seemed ecstatic over the attention and realized that it must give them both pleasure.

He wasn't particularly happy over that discovery and realized that, in the back of his mind, he'd thought the situation between himself and Jane totally unique, that she enjoyed *him*. Now it began to appear as if the females of her tribe simply enjoyed the mating act as much as the males did.

Feeling oddly deflated, he was on the point of moving on when one of the females seized the male's phallus and shoved it into her mouth. His heart skipped a beat. Instead of screaming in agony, however, as the female ate his phallus, the male looked as if he would pass out from the pleasure.

Grabbing the other female, he buried his face against her mound.

Ja-rael was certain he should have been revolted. Somehow, he wasn't. In fact, he grew uncomfortably aroused watching them.

Glancing around self-consciously, he moved away from the window, far more confused than he had been before he'd decided to search for Jane's tribe. He saw others as he moved around the docile, young, old, and in between, some in pairs--only the one threesome--many completely alone.

He did not see a single infant or even a young child.

That disturbed him even more than what he'd witnessed in the first room and he made the rounds a second time. Finally, in a darkened room, he saw a tiny bed that seemed to indicate at least one child.

He left then, returning to the ship when he realized he'd been gone far longer than he'd intended, but he was more disturbed than ever.

Chapter Six

Exhausted as she was from expending herself on Ja-rael, Elise had wildly erotic dreams much of the night. When she finally drifted gently toward consciousness again, the sense of well being that had surrounded her like a cocoon began to dissipate and anxiety took its place.

It took her some time to figure out why she was anxious. When memory finally filtered through her sluggish brain, she woke fully and sat up, looking around nervously for the alien that had abducted her and seemed to be laboring under the impression that he'd found himself a mate.

Finding herself alone, Elise slipped from the pallet and tiptoed to the door.

It was locked.

Frustrated, she pounded on it with her fist.

The only response was a strange noise from the deck below.

Wondering if the alien had captured other females, she lay down on the deck, rapping the surface with her knuckles, and then listening intently with her ear against the metal panel.

The sound she heard that time was definitely animal, not intelligent life.

That explained the smell.

Before she could scramble to her feet, the door of the cabin opened. Embarrassed for no apparent reason, Elise jumped up. "You locked me in!" she said accusingly.

He was carrying a container of some sort in each hand. He looked uncomfortable. "I wanted to ensure your safety, Jane."

"Right!" Elise snapped, then frowned. "Why are you calling me Jane?"

He tilted his head curiously. "You said that was your name."

"I did not," Elise said indignantly.

His lips tightened at her tone. "When you called me Tarzan."

"But … never mind. Call me Jane if you want to, just call me gone! It's been fun. I really enjoyed it, but I have to get back now."

Closing the door firmly behind him, he set the containers he held on a table and moved toward her.

Elise eyed him warily and took a few steps back.

He stopped. "What is your name?"

Elise studied him for several moments, but she really didn't see the harm in telling him her name. "Elise Dampier."

"Leez?"

"E-lise."

He couldn't pronounce it. She didn't know why she thought it was so cute the way he struggled with the unfamiliar sounds. Resolutely, she dismissed it. He wasn't cute. He was a big, scary alien and it didn't matter if he could fuck like a god. He'd kidnapped her. "My people will come for me if you don't let me go!"

"They are not. I checked."

"Those lazy fucking assholes! They probably haven't even missed me yet." They'd done a daily head count when they had first landed on Tor, but that was one security measure that had long since been disposed of. The climate was miserable, but there didn't seem to be any particular threat, and they'd fallen into a grim routine of survival.

He looked confused when she switched to English.

"You may as well let me go. I'm of absolutely no use to you."

A mixture of amusement and irritation gleamed in his eyes. "We are mated."

"Will you stop with the mating thing, damn it! We are *not* mated! We can't be mated. Can't you see I'm not even the same species as you are? Even if I wanted to, its really doubtful that it would work--if you're talking offspring here, and that's what it sounds like to me."

"Why do you say that?"

Elise looked at him. He sounded genuinely surprised. "Did you miss the part where I told you I was from Earth? It's another world on the other side of the universe. Do you know what the odds are that we'd be physiologically compatible? Astronomical, that's what!"

Frowning, he stepped closer to her. Grasping her wrist, he lifted her arm, studying it, studying her hand. Flattening his own hand, he fit their palms and fingers together. Elise swallowed convulsively, feeling a flutter low in her belly. "I see a female made as I am. I see a female whose body fits mine so cunningly they could not help but be made for one another," he said huskily.

The heat washed over her again. This time, however, Elise had time to realize that it was directly associated with his arousal. The very instant he became aroused, even slightly, her body reacted, even if he was yards from where she was standing. As crazy as it seemed, she realized it had to be the pheromones his body produced.

She couldn't imagine why any race would need to produce such powerful pheromones only to attract a mate, but it very obviously wasn't confined to attracting only females of their own kind.

It didn't particularly help to know that. The reaction was nothing she could control. Worse, whether her conscious mind had accepted him or not, her body had. It sang every time he rang the bell.

She fought the onslaught of drugging passion anyway, pulling away, taking another step back.

She had a bad feeling that she could've felt that powerful pull if she'd been at the habitat and wondered idly if it would draw every female the way it had her. The idea wasn't particularly pleasing. In fact, it was downright displeasing.

What was she thinking?

She shouldn't care one way or the other.

She didn't.

To her surprise, relief, and complete disappointment, the pheromoncs bombarding her with lust began to dissipate.

"You will grow accustomed," he said tightly and with that, departed, locking the door behind him.

Elise wilted to the pallet, too weak kneed to stand.

Everything on her body was throbbing with unrequited lust.

"Damn it!"

When she'd recovered a little, she got off the pallet and began banging on the door again. "We can talk about this! We're two rational human … uh … beings!"

No response.

"I'm not going anywhere with you, damn it!"

Still no response.

After a little while she heard movement below her and the animals began making more noise. Moving to the only porthole the cabin boasted, she plastered her face against it, peering down at the hull of the ship. After a few moments, a large hatch opened and a small herd of really strange looking animals emerged. Carrying some sort of device, Ja-rael emerged behind them. As two of the creatures broke from the pack and headed for the jungle, he fired it and a bolt of blue lightening arched from it. The 'fingers' dug into the ground to one side of the animals. Shrieking, they instantly changed direction, heading back toward the main group.

It took some maneuvering, but after a few minutes, he had the animals in a tight little wad, heading in the direction he wanted.

The creatures reminded her of a child's rendering of an ostrich--boxy body, four legs, long, snake like neck and what appeared to be tiny wings. From her position, they seemed to have feathers, as well. She couldn't tell much about the heads, but it didn't look as if they had beaks. Birds with lips.

Really strange.

She wondered where he was going with them.

It didn't matter. All that mattered was he was gone, and likely to be gone a while if he was, as she guessed, taking the animals to trade with the Torrines.

Moving away from the porthole, she began searching the room for something she might use to crack the lock on the door. In the process, she discovered he'd brought her food and water.

She knew the water was safe--was fairly certain, anyway. She wasn't so sure about the food. He might have put something in it. Even if he hadn't, she might find it totally disgusting--and for that matter it might not be something her physiology could handle.

It smelled pretty good, though, and she was starving. She'd been hungry when she left the habitat the day before and she hadn't had anything since.

Grabbing the containers up, she moved to the bed and tried the meat-like substance. It was meat and it tasted wonderful. She ate it all and licked her fingers, but by the time she'd finished she was so full she felt like she was going to explode. She lay down, groaning, wondering if there'd been something wrong with the food after all.

The misery subsided after a little while and she realized she'd just eaten too much too fast. Climbing off the pallet, she moved to the door and examined the mechanism. It wasn't an electronic lock. It was mechanical.

She turned the entire cabin upside down searching for something small enough to slide through the crack that would also be strong enough to manipulate the lock. She found the head, which was a great relief, but aside from that the only thing she discovered in the search was that, from the layer of dust that coated everything, Ja-rael obviously spent very little time in the cabin, and that the ship spent most of its time in dock. There were no personal belongings beyond a couple of robes and several more loincloths like the one he was wearing. The robes were lightweight and virtually sheer. Shrugging, Elise donned one. As little as it covered, she still felt better, somewhat protected, and it was too light to make much difference in the temperature comfort level, particularly inside the ship, which had some environmental control.

When the search turned up nothing suitable for trying to pick the lock, she examined the contents of the cabin for anything that she might use to force it, or pry the door open.

The pallet lay directly on the floor without any sort of frame. Aside from the pallet, there was only the one small table. She didn't know what the table was made of, but it was either bolted to the floor, or it was the heaviest thing she'd ever tried to lift.

Tired from the effort, feeling anxious and vaguely hysterical, she flung herself down on the pallet, glaring at the door. Unfortunately, she didn't have the power to burn a hole through it with her rage. Eventually, her emotional level dropped and she began to glance idly around the room again.

Her gaze lit on the containers he'd left and the utensils he'd given her to eat with.

"Moron!" she berated herself, jumping to her feet and grabbing up the blade.

She'd worked up a sweat by the time she managed to jimmy the lock, but triumph filled her. Without pause, she headed down the corridor. She'd already run past the gangplank before she realized she'd missed it. Backtracking, she studied the mechanism for several nerve wracking minutes and finally figured it out by trial and error. She'd been too preoccupied with the alien when he'd used it to retrieve the gangplank to remember what he'd done with any accuracy.

The moment the porthole opened and the plank began to descend she began scrambling down the gangplank. In her haste, she slid off the end, shredding the damned robe and landing on her ass in the gravelly soil. Hopping up at once, she glanced around and made for the woods as fast as she could.

She was shaking by the time she reached the cover of the forest. Instinct told her she should simply run without looking back, but she couldn't resist the need to know whether he'd seen her escape.

She was sorry she'd spared the time because she caught a glimpse of movement at the edge of the field and she had a bad feeling it was Ja-rael and it wasn't going to be many minutes before he discovered his 'prize' had escaped.

Chapter Seven

For possibly the first time in her life, Elise discovered that luck was on her side. It was a good thing, too, because common sense had abandoned her.

She was already headed in the right direction, though, and she had a fair head start. If her luck held, maybe she could reach the habitat before he discovered she was gone and ....

Maybe she could get far enough he wouldn't think it was worth the risk?

It took every ounce of common sense she could muster to make herself jog instead of running as fast as she could. She knew, though, that the heat and humidity would strike her down if she tried to run all out and she wouldn't get far at all.

Fortunately, the path was well marked, fairly level and free of obstacles.

She'd made it all the way back to the creek when Ja-rael sprang out of the woods like a--like an enormous jungle cat. She screamed like a banshee when he leapt out at her, more because she was startled and actually thought it was some sort of man eater than because she realized it was him.

Fortunately, the adrenaline rush acted on her like a goose in the ass instead of draining every ounce of strength from her. She left the ground by a good two feet, and hit it again running, throwing up dirt, clods of grass, and pebbles.

She'd made it all the way around the little pool before he tackled her. The collision propelled them both into the stream and the chill of the water after the heat she'd generated took her breath. By the time she'd stopped coughing and sputtering, she was hanging limply over his shoulder and headed back the way she'd just run.

"Jesus fucking Christ! You scared the ever loving shit out of me!" she growled, bracing her hands on his back and rearing upwards.

"You ran," he said in Torrine. "Why?"

Elise glared down at him, too angry for several moments to come up with the words she needed even to speak to him. "Put me down!" she demanded at last.

To her surprise, he complied immediately. Glaring at her, he shook his finger in her face, as if she was a child. "It is not safe for my lioness to go without escort."

Elise felt her jaw drop. "You're not serious!" she demanded indignantly.

His eyes narrowed. "You are mine now. I will keep you safe."

Slapping his finger aside, she poked him in the chest with her finger. "I'm not yours, you big ... overgrown ... cat!"

He frowned suspiciously. "What is this word?"

Elise opened her mouth and then shut it again, deciding it might not be a good idea to teach him English. "Unimportant!" she said finally. "The important thing is, I'm not yours!"

His eyes narrowed. "You mated with me. You can not un-accept me now!" he growled.

"Oh yes I can!"

"Can not! It is law!"

Elise gaped at him. "Now wait just a damned minute! I'm not a Torrine and I don't give a damn what your laws are! I'm going back to the habitat."

Stepping away from him, she went around him and stalked toward the pool once more. He followed her. It was too much to hope he'd give up so easily.

"I have the bride price."

"And that means exactly zero to me, buddy!"

"What is this speak you use? I do not understand," he said, irritation in his voice.

"English."

"An-leez?"

She didn't bother trying to correct his pronunciation. "The language of my people. I told you, we aren't the same. I'm not ... lioness, or a Torrine, or a Meeri. I'm from Earth and we speak English--uh --spoke English in my country there and we still speak it here because it's *our* language."

"You speak Torrine badly. I will teach you Meeri."

Elise glared at him. "No you won't, because you're not going to be around to teach it to me. Go home!"

He said nothing for several moments, but he continued to keep step with her.

"Why are you following me?" Elise snapped.

"I must stay with my mate," he said doggedly.

"I don't want you!" Elise snapped in exasperation and then was instantly sorry.

Hurt flickered over his expression and then disappeared, replaced with determination. "This is untrue."

"Don't throw that up to me," Elise snapped, embarrassed. "I couldn't help it. It's that … thing you have. I mean …." She stopped blushing even harder. "I didn't mean thing as in *thing*. I meant … Oh, to hell with it!"

"I will learn An-leez."

In spite of all she could do, empathy began to seep through her. He was sweet--misguided--but sweet. "It won't make a difference."

"I will know what you say when you begin to shout and mutter in this strange speak."

She gave him a look. So much for being anxious to please. When she glanced away from him, Elise discovered that she didn't see anything that looked familiar. She stopped walking and looked around. "Where the hell am I?"

Ja-rael stopped as well, looking around. "In the forest."

She gave him another drop dead look. "I know I'm in the damned forest, you ass!"

"What is azz?"

She could tell from his expression that he'd figured out it wasn't a compliment. "You let me walk the wrong way," she said accusingly.

"I only follow to protect."

She could see he was trying very hard to hide his amusement. Despite everything, it charmed her, and then sent a jolting realization through her.

He *was* alien, but he was a being the same as she was, and most likely fully capable of understanding, and feeling, pretty much everything she experienced. She'd hurt his feelings with her childish outburst before. As difficult as she found it to believe that he'd no more than set eyes on her before he'd become enthralled with her, it was hard to dispute his behavior.

She couldn't help but be warmed by the thought.

She dismissed it immediately.

Alien or not, he was damned attractive, but he was still alien. It was a shame, really, because there wasn't a single male in the habitat that she found even vaguely interesting, but such was life. She was going to have to live with it and Ja-rael was going to have to live with it.

He'd be much better off with a female of his own kind. She just had to convince him she wasn't his kind.

For an intelligent being, he was pretty damned hard headed, though.

"Your tribe is this way," he said helpfully, pointing.

Elise studied him suspiciously for several moments, but once she'd examined the area of the forest he was pointing toward, she decided it did look familiar. Regardless, she was vaguely amazed when he led her directly to the habitat without any trouble at all.

She stopped at the edge of the fields. "Thanks! But I'm home now--and safe."

He frowned. "I have come to make things right," he said, his entire attitude uncompromising. "I will pay your bride price to your family, and then we must go. In another day, we will not be able to reach Meeri."

Chapter Eight

Elise stared at Ja-rael speechlessly. Obviously, alien or not, he was as single minded as any human male it had ever been her misfortune to tangle with. Glancing around a little helplessly while she sought patience, Elise saw that their arrival had attracted the attention of her fellow Earthlings. Most of those in the vicinity were merely gaping at Ja-rael. A small knot, led by their exalted leader, Kenneth Smith, were approaching cautiously.

Plunking her hands on her hips, she glared at Kenneth as he spoke.

"Is he dangerous?"

A little surprised by the question, Elise turned and looked Ja-rael over from an entirely different perspective. He was every bit of six foot four if he was an inch and his entire body was taut and lean with muscle. She blinked, realizing she hadn't actually considered him dangerous for even a moment--except for those moments when he'd leapt at her in the forest and she'd thought he was something else.

She frowned. "He seems very peaceful," she said a little doubtfully.

The two men behind Kenneth seemed to relax fractionally.

"What happened?" Kenneth demanded, his tone and attitude abruptly more commanding.

Elise narrowed her eyes at him. "If any of you assholes had come to look for me, you might have found that out yesterday!"

Kenneth flushed. "We took a small party out when you didn't come back. We found the basket. It looked like there'd been a struggle. We were afraid the habitat would be attacked. We withdrew for security purposes." He paused. "It's standard protocol."

"Are you the sire of Leez?" Ja-rael demanded, abruptly entering the conversation.

Kenneth gaped at him in outrage. "Do I look fucking old enough to be her father?"

"He doesn't understand English," Elise pointed out dryly. "No!"

Ja-rael's eyes narrowed at the curt response. "I would speak with her sire. I have business with him."

"What the hell is he babbling about?"

Elise couldn't prevent the blush that rose in her cheeks. "He thinks he can buy me for his ... uh ... mate. He wants to negotiate the bride price."

Kenneth's jaw sagged.

One of the men behind him, Sawyer, snickered. The other, Dickerson, reddened with anger. "Our women aren't for sale!" he growled challengingly.

Ja-rael focused on Dickerson and his entire demeanor changed in the blink of an eye. Every muscle in his body tensed, as if he would spring at the slightest movement. His voice, when he spoke, emerged as a low, rumbling, very threatening growl. "She is mine. I have claimed her. I am willing to do the honorable thing because I will not have my mate disgraced, but any who challenge me will die."

Every human within hearing range took a step back, including Elise. He caught her wrist and pulled her behind him.

Kenneth forced a sickly smile. "I think we just have a little misunderstanding here." He slid a glance at Elise and spoke English out of the corner of his mouth. "Is he alone?"

Elise, peering around Ja-rael's shoulder, merely stared at him. "Why?"

He bared his teeth in a parody of a smile. "Are ... we ... in ... imminent ... danger ... of ... an ... attack?" he asked, enunciating each word slowly.

Elise felt a chill go through her, felt as if she'd suddenly found herself standing on a precipice with crumbling rock beneath her feet. They felt threatened and people were dangerous and unpredictable when they were threatened. She simply stared at him for several moments, knowing she had to somehow diffuse the situation, to make Kenneth and the others feel less threatened. At the same time, she wasn't about to tell them that, so far as she knew, Ja-rael *was* alone. Their focus then would be on Ja-rael as the threat and they would see no reason not to make use of their overwhelming odds to handle the situation. "I don't think so," she finally responded cautiously. "There's not an army

of them waiting in the forest, if that's what you're asking.
But ... uh ... he's a chieftain of his people and I'm sure
they wouldn't take it well if he was attacked," she added,
lying baldly.

"What is he asking?" Ja-rael demanded abruptly.

Elise glanced up at Ja-rael guiltily. She forced a smile.
"He wanted to know if you would be willing to go inside
where we could negotiate this situation in a civilized
manner."

Ja-rael didn't look entirely convinced, but he nodded
decisively after only a slight hesitation. "I have shown
myself willing to negotiate."

Kenneth, sweating profusely now, his smile looking more
pained by the moment, nodded and gestured for them to
follow. When he turned back toward the habitat, he raised
his voice jovially. "We have a visitor, everyone. Let's all go
inside and make him welcome and offer refreshment."

For several moments, everyone merely gaped at him
blankly. Finally, after glancing anxiously at one another,
they began to move toward the habitat slowly.

Elise ground her teeth, tempted to strangle Kenneth. She
supposed she could see his point. He wasn't convinced that
there wasn't a threat and he wanted everyone boarded up
inside if there was, but it was easy to see that between Ja-
rael himself and Kenneth's nervous reassurances, everyone
was on the verge of panic.

She glanced at Ja-rael worriedly several times. She
couldn't honestly say he was harmless, despite the fact that
he hadn't offered her harm in any way. His species was
advanced enough to have space travel, but he also bore the
build of a fighter and not just the build for that matter.
When he'd felt threatened, he'd reacted instantly, like
someone accustomed to reacting to violent aggression.

On the other hand, she had no reason to believe he had
any intention of doing anything beyond protecting himself.

On impulse, she slipped her hand into his and laced her
fingers through his. He glanced down at her with a mixture
of surprise and pleasure, smiling faintly, one brow lifting
questioningly.

She smiled back at him and then glanced around
surreptitiously at the others to gauge their reaction. They'd

noticed the gesture and some of the tension seemed to be dissipating.

It was blessedly cool inside the habitat after the heat of the late afternoon and everyone seemed to relax a good deal more, moving almost gaily toward the dining hall where everyone gathered for meals. Once her eyes had adjusted to the dark interior, Elise saw that those with kitchen duty had already begun preparing for the evening meal. They looked up in surprise and not a little irritation to see everyone filing in early, but apparently decided they had the time wrong, for they began to move more quickly in setting up.

Ja-rael flinched when the evening bell sounded, glancing around sharply. Elise squeezed his hand and released it. "It's OK. That's just the dinner bell, calling everyone in to eat."

He sent her a curious look, but seemed to dismiss it, examining the people and his surroundings with interest. His curiosity prompted Elise to actually look at the habitat for the first time in a very long time. She was both surprised and embarrassed, seeing it now through the eyes of a stranger.

The habitat was painfully utilitarian. It was kept scrupulously clean, but there was nothing even approaching aesthetic beauty about it. She, like everyone else, had been too busy with the business of surviving to take much note of her surroundings, but she supposed, in a sense they all had.

Small wonder everyone was so depressed considering their surroundings. There was no beauty, nothing 'homey' about it, nothing even actually 'personal.' She had a few personal effects in her quarters, but very little. She doubted anyone else had much more than she did. They hadn't been allowed to bring more than they could carry in two bags, which had left no room for anything but absolute necessities and not even much of that. She'd brought a few mementos, but she'd almost regretted even the little she had brought. They belonged to another world, another life and only made the exile even harder to bear.

They were never going home again.

Shying away from the pang that thought caused her, Elise focused instead on showing Ja-rael where to find the tray and utensils as the service crew began serving the evening meal. Even that caused her a pang, however. It gave the meal an institutionalized atmosphere. It was practical, the only sensible way to provide for so many, but it still made her feel more like a prisoner than a member of a working society.

Kenneth directed them toward his table, unsettling two from their usual seats to go and search for another place to perch. It was patently obvious, however, that no one was especially anxious to sit with their visitor. Kenneth's wife, upon discovering that the only free chair left at the table was next to Ja-rael, looked around the room a little helplessly, as if someone would rush over and rescue her from sitting next to the 'beast'. Elise regretted taking the seat across from him then. She glared at Maude pointedly for several moments. Maude gave her a superior glance down her nose and finally settled, muttering under her breath about savages with loincloths.

"You're right," Elise put in. "He should dress for dinner like we all do."

Maude reddened at the sarcasm. "He might at least have freshened up a bit."

Elise had to fight the urge to counter the insult with something really nasty. The heat and humidity was awful, but she'd been closer to Ja-rael than any of the others. She knew damned well he didn't stink. "Sorry. That's probably me. I missed my tea cup bath."

Water was rationed. They all did their best to maintain good hygiene, but it was difficult to say the least when they were only allowed two liters of water per day for that purpose. They'd already had one well dry up. For months, until they'd managed to get a new well dug and run the pipes, everyone had had to go down to the stream and lug water back for bathing, cooking, and drinking. No one wanted to experience the misery of doing completely without running water again so they grumbled beneath their breath at the primitive conditions, but they stuck to the rations they were allowed.

Kenneth cleared his throat before Maude could think of a come back, giving both his wife and Elise an admonishing look. Maude was effectively silenced--as usual. Elise merely glared back at him. Finally, realizing he wasn't going to be able to cow her with a look, he glanced at Ja-rael. "You seem to have a different accent than the other Torrines I've spoken to. Not from around here?"

Ja-rael's face tightened. It would have been obvious to a block of wood that he found it insulting to be thought a Torrine.

She could see it went right over Kenneth's head.

"I am not Torrine. I am Meeri."

"Oh? Is that far from here?"

When Ja-rael named the distance, Kenneth's jaw dropped. "But ... but the *whole* planet isn't that big! I must be confused about the units of measurement."

"Meeri is the sister world to Torrine."

Kenneth's chair made a screeching noise as he pushed back from the table to stare at Ja-rael. "I beg your pardon? Did you say 'sister world'?"

"It's another planet," Elise said helpfully.

"You mean to say he thinks he's from another planet?" Kenneth demanded, forgetting to switch back to English.

Ja-rael gave him a look. "I do not think it. I know it."

Kenneth turned an unbecoming shade of red. "Oh! I beg your pardon! I didn't realize I'd spoken in Torrine."

"It makes it so much better for him to think we're insulting him every time we speak English," Elise said dryly.

Kenneth ignored the rebuke. "But there isn't another habitable planet in this system."

"How would we know that?" Elise demanded. "We were all in the hyber units when the computer made the decision to land."

He gave her a look as if she were an imbecile. "I've been over the logs. This is the first planet our ship came upon that was within the parameters we preset."

"Which doesn't rule out that there is another world in this system. Besides, I know he's telling the truth. I've been on his ship. I can't say that I examined it all that closely, but I know an interplanetary cruiser when I see one."

Kenneth turned to study Ja-rael as if seeing him for the first time. She knew what was running through his mind. They'd all immediately jumped to the conclusion that he was some sort of primitive--because of his clothing. It was absurd to base an assumption on so little. After all, if anyone had stumbled upon the lot of them, they would probably have thought the same thing.

Actually, upon consideration, she wasn't so sure they could even claim to be members of a technologically advanced civilization anymore. They had a hell of a time even fixing the toilets in this heap.

"Hey! You think it might be that moon we only see occasionally?" Sawyers, who was sitting just beyond Kenneth, exclaimed on sudden insight. "I thought it was a strange phenomcnon."

Elise could see the gears turning in Kenneth's brain and she wasn't sure she liked the turn things had taken. She hated Torrine as badly as the next person, but there was no way they were ever going to get their ship off the ground again, and who was to say Meeri was any better anyway? Besides, they'd already put a lot of time and effort into carving out a place for themselves here. She wasn't so sure anyone had the energy to start over from scratch somewhere else. She was pretty damned sure she didn't.

When he spoke, she saw she'd read him precisely.

"This Meeri--is it like this world?"

Ja-rael's expression went perfectly blank. He glanced at Elise. "Why?"

Kenneth forced a laugh. "Just curious. I figured we should get to know a little something about each others' culture ... and so forth."

Elise was embarrassed. One moment everyone was acting as if something nasty had fallen into their swimming pool, and the next they were suggesting going with the 'nasty' to join him in his pool. Ja-rael knew it, too. It was just as obvious that he wasn't enchanted with the idea now that he'd gotten the chance to get to know her 'tribe' a little better.

Ja-rael frowned thoughtfully. "You said that you were not the sire of Leez ."

Kenneth forced another laugh. "The customs. You see, that's just what I was talking about. We do things a little differently. From what you said, I gather your own customs on Meeri must be very similar to those practiced by the Torrine."

Ja-rael studied the cooling food on his plate, but Elise doubted he had much interest in it. He'd eaten very little--

probably because it was the next thing to inedible--his manners, however, whatever his customs, were far better than those practiced by most of the people she came in daily contact with.

She had the feeling that he was considering his next move, partly because he'd already displayed that he could be extraordinarily single minded, and partly because he was obviously uncomfortable about Kenneth's interest in his home world.

"Why do you think it is strange that I come from a world other than this one when Leez has told me that you have traveled here from a world far away?"

Kenneth turned red, opened and closed his mouth several times and finally managed a smile that looked more like a grimace. "It's just that we hadn't met anyone before except the Torrine people. And then, too, from what I was able to discern from the ship's onboard computers, this was determined to be the only habitable planet in this system."

"This is truth, then? Your people traveled here from another galaxy?"

Kenneth shrugged. "Sadly, yes. Mankind's first, and unfortunately, last, venture beyond their solar system. We were fortunate we were ready to take the next step. We had colonies spread throughout the system, but we hadn't harnessed the speed we needed to go beyond--not within a reasonable time span. When our mother world became dangerously destabilized, we had spread out as far as we could reach. The meteor pretty well finished it off, but the worst of it was that, when Earth was destroyed, it destabilized the entire system. Those who could evacuated into the great unknown, hopeful our ships would carry us to other worlds where we could live ... and we are grateful every day that we found this one and the Torrines have been kind enough to allow us to stay."

Ja-rael turned and looked directly at Elise. His expression was carefully neutral, but she knew he realized that what she'd told him was the truth. Oddly enough, the realization saddened her. He'd thought that she was beautiful. He said she took his breath away. No one, in her entire life, had ever told her she was beautiful.

But he'd thought so because he'd thought she was the same species as he was.

She couldn't begin to imagine how he felt now, or what was going through his mind.

She should've just been relieved. At least now he understood why she wouldn't let him claim her as his mate and cart her off to another world.

"This habitat," Kenneth said rather loudly, and expansively, "is a perfect representation of our technology at its finest. You wouldn't know it to look at it, I know, but this is actually the ship that brought us here--and it's truly an engineering marvel, designed for intergalactic travel, and once the perfect place is located, the ship converts with very little effort into a habitat.

"Of course, it did take a bit more effort than we'd expected. Engineers, you know--always assuming everyone else can figure out what they had in mind-- and the directions were confusing as hell--but it's sound, secure, and quite comfortable."

Ja-rael didn't even bother to glance around. His gaze remained on her and Elise felt something stir to life.

Desire.

Dread.

She clenched her hands in her lap, wondering if anyone around her had noticed, feeling dread keep pace with growing desire, trying without much success to fight off the lethargy that was stealing through her.

She was going to embarrass herself and everyone else if she didn't do something to distract Ja-rael.

It was as she was looking around a little frantically for inspiration that she happened to notice that Maude was looking Ja-rael over with interest. She'd ceased to eat and was merely toying with her fork. Her eyes were slightly unfocused.

Elise blinked. She knew that glazed look.

Even as it dawned upon her that Ja-rael's pheromones weren't just bombarding her, but Maude, as well, Maude dropped her fork and began to walk her fingers across the table toward Ja-rael's arm.

Glancing around, Elise saw that every female at every table around them had begun to fan themselves and look around, as if searching for a target for the desire they, too, were feeling. A mixture of possessiveness and anxiety filtered through her own desire along with the sudden realization that half the women in the habitat were going to be curled around Ja-rael in moments, fighting over who was going to mount him first if she didn't do something quickly.

"Oh my God!" she exclaimed at that thought, jumping to her feet and knocking Ja-rael's beverage glass over, sending the chilled water spilling into his lap. He gasped, leaping to his feet so quickly his chair overturned.

"What the hell?" Kenneth exclaimed, breaking off his monologue.

"I'll take care of it!" Elise said a little breathlessly, scurrying quickly around the table. Grasping Ja-rael's wrist, she tugged him behind her, heading for the nearest exit with no clear idea of what she intended beyond removing Ja-rael from the mob of women that was likely to assault him at any moment.

Chapter Nine

Either the cold water dampened Ja-rael's ardor, or panic supplanted Elise's. She managed to make it out of the dining hall without incident. By the time she'd reached the corridor, however, she couldn't think far beyond the need that was burning inside of her. She felt dizzy, dehydrated, shaky and weak kneed, almost ill. Without a word, she turned down the corridor, still dragging Ja-rael behind her, and headed for her quarters--which thankfully were only one level up.

She had to key the code three times before she managed to get it right. Tugging Ja-rael inside, she slammed the door and began rubbing against him, moaning in pleasure to at last feel his flesh against her own.

"Now?" Ja-rael asked, his voice gravelly with desire.

The sound of his desire made her belly clench. "Yes. Right now," Elise demanded breathlessly, trying to pull the robe off, remove his loincloth, and rub herself against him all at the same time.

He caught her shoulders, pushing her a little away. "We should not. We have settled nothing."

"We'll talk later," Elise murmured, straining toward him and licking a path along his chest to his neck. A dizzying rush went through her as she tasted him on her tongue, felt his taste and scent flow through her veins like a euphoria drug.

A shudder went through him. He shook his head, obviously trying to tamp his own desire. "You are not a maned lioness."

"I'll be one if you want me to," Elise muttered distractedly. "Just give it to me. I need you inside of me."

His fingers tightened on her shoulders. He shook her slightly. "You can not be what you are not."

Elise looked up at him at that, trying to figure out why he wasn't cooperating. Dimly, she realized that Ja-rael was striving for a rational conversation-- which she should *want* to take part in. She felt, however, like someone who's had just enough alcohol not to give a damn about anything beyond her focus at the moment--which was stuffing his cock inside of her as quickly as she could get her hands on it. "Not now," she said through gritted teeth. "I can't think when you do this to me. Fuck me now. We'll talk later."

Something flickered in Ja-rael's eyes, something she couldn't begin to read in her current state. "I have done nothing beyond desire you."

"Yes," Elise gasped. "That's it. I've never experienced anything like it. It sets me on fire. I feel it the moment you do. Smell it. Taste it."

"Do you?"

"Mmm," Elise murmured, stroking her hands down his belly and trying to dig beneath his loincloth.

He held her and stepped away, just out of her reach, studying her for several moments as if trying to make up his mind about something. "You will be my lioness?"

"Yes. Anything. Right now."

Ja-rael looked at the bunk, then glanced down at her again, struggling with the urge to move toward it and give in to the desire she was feeding in him. "You will be my mate?"

"Yes! Right now!" Elise gasped. "The bed, the floor--Ja-rael! Please. I need you."

"My ship?"

That question penetrated the heated fog of her brain. "Ship? Ok. The ship. But first here."

"No."

It took Elise several moments for that word to translate in her brain. She looked at him beseechingly. "But--I *need* it," she said plaintively.

He looked torn for several moments. Finally, he pulled her tightly against him, enfolding her in his arms. Elise stiffened at the unexpected gesture, but then relaxed against him as she felt his heat and scent permeate her body, weaving itself along every nerve ending, soothing the need and at the same time feeding the fire.

"I desire you, my beautiful Leez … so much I am almost ill with it, but I need more. I need a companion. I want my own cubs." He hesitated for many moments. "… and I do not think you can give that to me. We are much the same, but very different also, maybe too different."

His sense of despair invaded the heated glow that enveloped her and Elise stroked his back soothingly. "But-- this is good. This is *very* good," she pointed out.

He pulled away to look down at her. When he did, Elise went up on her tiptoes and nuzzled his neck, stroking her cheek along his jaw, seeking his lips. She couldn't quite reach them and, to her consternation, he didn't immediately close the distance that separated them. She placed nibbling kisses along his jaw and chin and then offered her lips to him once more.

He hesitated so long, she thought he would not take her offering at all. As if he couldn't quite prevent himself from doing so, he moved closer, finally brushing his lips lightly along hers. Sighing with pleasure, Elise molded her lips against his hard mouth.

He opened his mouth over hers then, thrusting his tongue past her unresisting lips and plunging ruthlessly inside the warm, sensitive cavern of her mouth. Elise moaned, feeling her body quake in a minute release that made darkness swarm through her mind as his tongue made love to hers, stroking along it, entwining with hers. Weakness swept through her and then desire stronger than before. She dug her fingers into the hard flesh of his muscular back, pressing more tightly against him as the heat surged through her in dizzying waves. When she found that that wasn't enough, she slipped her hands down along his back and dug her fingers into his buttocks, rocking against him rhythmically.

He tore his mouth from hers, gasping hoarsely, staring down at her with an expression Elise found impossible to decipher, shook his head slowly as he gasped for breath. "I am as bound to you as you are to me. There will not be another for me," he said harshly, his voice raw, hoarse.

He caught her jaw in the palm of his hand, squeezing until she lifted her heavy eyelids and looked directly at him. "You will be my mate?"

Elise nodded.

"Say it!"

"Yes! Let's do it now."

His lips tightened. "At the ship."

Elise blinked. He was back to that again? "But first here."

He shook his head. Pushing her away, he grasped her hand and led her out the door and down the corridor. It took every ounce of concentration she could muster just to manage putting one foot in front of the other or Elise would have protested loudly and very vocally. She hardly knew how or even when they left the habitat, had no idea at all of whether they passed anyone along the way, only became aware after some moments that it was too dark to see. When she stumbled for the third time, Ja-rael stopped and pulled her against him. Kissing her briefly, he swung her into his arms and set off at a jolting lope that made it impossible for Elise to manage much more than to cling to him. She nuzzled her face along his neck anyway, relishing his scent.

His ears fascinated her, she remembered, and when she realized she couldn't coax him into kissing her again, she wove a path in that direction with her lips. He almost dropped her, letting out a sound that was part growl of desperation, part groan of despair,

when she explored the sensitive cavity with her tongue.

"Cease!" he growled. "Or I will disgrace myself by spilling my seed now and have nothing for you."

Momentarily subdued by that threat, Elise went back to nuzzling his neck and stroking her hands over every part of him that she could reach. The soft down that covered his head fascinated her and she contented herself for some time with exploring the feel of it and the shape of his skull. It seemed to take far too long to reach the ship, however, and impatience drove her to explore his ear again. "Let's stop here ... just for a few minutes," she whispered into his ear. "I ache for you. Just touch me, kiss me."

He slowed, nuzzling his face against hers. Coming to a stop, he covered her mouth, kissing her all too briefly before he pulled away with a groan. "Temptress," he muttered. "I won't be able to stop."

"We can fuck all night if you like," she murmured hopefully.

She heard him grinding his teeth together. Before she could think of anything to do to stack the odds in her favor, however, he switched from a jog to a run. The jostling made it impossible for her to do anything besides hang on at first. It occurred to her after several minutes that he was amazingly strong--inhumanly strong. His muscular physique had implied that he was, of course, but he'd been carrying her for--she had no idea, only that it seemed to be a very long time.

Moreover, he moved through the darkness as if it were broad daylight, more surefooted than she was even in the light of day.

Those thoughts brought the differences between their two species home to her as nothing else. No man could do what he was doing. She stiffened, trying to pierce the dark and get her bearings, wondering just how far they were from the habitat.

Had he simply walked out of the habitat with her without anyone offering any challenge at all?

Try though she might, she couldn't recall seeing anyone. Perhaps they'd all still been in the dining hall? Many of them, no doubt, wondering what had come over them to cause them to behave so strangely unlike themselves.

She knew what had caused it, however.

"Where are you taking me?" she finally asked, trying not to sound hostile.

Ja-rael stopped abruptly. Catching a fistful of her hair, he tipped her head back and kissed her aggressively, his mouth forcing her lips to part. Elise tried to resist the lure, but the moment he thrust his tongue into her mouth, her will turned to mist. She felt as if she were falling down the throat of an inferno. Fire erupted along her nerve endings, exploded deep in her core.

When she went limp with desire, he pulled away and began to move once more.

Disappointment filled her. She needed to feel more than the heated thrust of his tongue. She needed to feel his huge cock forcing its way along her channel, stroking her, filling her whole world.

The sound of his feet landing on a metallic surface filtered into her heated mind. She would have fallen when he set her on her feet except that he kept an arm around her as he worked the system to retract the gangplank and close the hatch. A mechanical whir filled her ears and then dizziness swept over her as he swung her into his arms again and moved down the corridor.

Her stomach went momentarily weightless as he leaned to drop her gently onto the mattress of his bed. Coolness filtered through the thin fabric that covered her back, and then heat along her breasts, belly and thighs as his body settled over hers with a delightful heaviness. He kissed her. Covering her mouth hungrily, he explored the sensitive inner flesh of her mouth with a thoroughness that made every breath a struggle, his hands moving over her with restless possessiveness all the while, tugging at the robe until he'd stripped it away, pulling at his own clothing until he'd discarded that, as well. Then nothing lay between them and she could feel the smooth roughness of his skin rubbing against hers in delightful abrasion. She could feel the heat and hardness of his cock digging into her belly. She rocked her hips, nudging her mound against his erection. The pressure only made her ache worse, however, and she struggled to spread her thighs so that she could feel him nestled into her cleft.

He had her legs pinned beneath his, making it impossible for her to move more than a few inches. Lifting his lips from hers, he shifted so that he could look down at her. Feeling his gaze, she lifted her eyelids with a tremendous effort and gazed up at him with reproach.

"You know you are mine. Your body calls to me, responds to my need for you," he murmured harshly.

"Mmm," she moaned. "Yes. I need you inside of me."

"I can not break this bond that chains me to you even if it was my wish, and I can't find the strength in me to wish it."

Elise licked her lips, not at all certain what he was talking about beyond his own desire. Lifting her hand, she stroked his chest and belly, seeking blindly for his cock and coming up empty. She couldn't reach it. He held her when she would have shifted lower to gasp his turgid flesh. "You don't want to," she reminded him. "You want to …," she hesitated, deciding to use the word he seemed to prefer. "…mate with me."

His eyes slid half closed. He studied her broodingly for several moments and finally leaned down and blazed a trail of fire along her flesh with his lips and tongue, moving along her throat to her collar bone and then down between her breasts. He hesitated in the valley and then nibbled a path up the slope to the peak of one breast. Her nipple tightened almost painfully at his approach, her pulse beating out a pounding ache.

The pleasure was so intense when the heat of his mouth closed around the tight, aching bud, that she cried out, arching her back upward. He released her at once, lifting his head to look at her in surprise and consternation. She dug her fingers into his arm, urging him wordlessly to touch her again. After a moment, he caught the nipple between his lips, sucked experimentally. Groaning, Elise clasped him to her, mindlessly stroking the back of his head as her body scaled the heights to culmination in a dizzying rush.

The tension broke, dragging a cry from her as her body convulsed with it. She hadn't even fallen completely from the heights when he moved to her other breast and suckled it as he had the first.

Heat surged inside of her again, tension coiling in every muscle. Elise moved beneath him, unable to remain still, stroking his body feverishly. Apparently encouraged by her reaction, or driven by his own needs, he began a restless quest to explore every inch of her body with his mouth and tongue, moving down over her belly to her navel, then up again to the other breast. Teasing that sensitive bud until she was moaning incessantly, he wove a path downward, past her navel and nuzzled his face against her mound.

Elise gasped, clutching at him, but offered no resistance as he caught her legs beneath her knees and spread her thighs. His cheek grazed her inner thigh as he leaned toward her, sending a shiver of anticipation through her, making her heart clutch painfully. The warmth of his breath whispered across the curls that covered her mound, making her belly clench in expectation. When she felt the heat and slight abrasiveness of his tongue parting her nether lips and gliding curiously along her cleft, she gasped, gripping the covers beneath her as she arched upward to meet the pleasure his touch promised. His lips nipped at the tiny, exquisitely sensitive bud of her clit and then he opened his mouth over it and her heart almost seemed to stop as she felt the heat and pull of his mouth.

"Oh! Ja-rael," she murmured on an ecstatic groan. "That feels so good."

She realized in the next moment that she'd spoken in her own tongue, not Torrine, but he seemed to need no interpretation. Settling more firmly between her thighs, he lavished his attentions upon her until she screamed with release, bucking against him as her body convulsed in almost painful spasms of rapture. When her cries had died to hoarse whimpers, he lifted his head at last, shifted upward, nibbling heated kisses along her body as he advanced.

His kisses brought her body to attention once more. By the time he'd settled to teasing her breasts again, her mind was a drugged morass of passion, the fever upon her, coiling tighter and tighter. She reached for him when he rose above her at last, spreading her thighs wider. She shifted to meet him as she felt the questing head of his cock slipping along her cleft, gathering the moisture that collected there to ease his possession.

She held herself still, held her breath at his first thrusting incursions along her passage, lifting in counter to his thrusts until his cock had possessed her fully, so deeply she felt him almost as a part of herself, but delightfully separate, as well.

As he sought the rhythm he needed to find his own pleasure, she felt her passions rising once more toward yet another crisis, more slowly this time, more intensely with the feel of her body wrapped around the length of his cock. She squeezed her eyes tightly, holding the sensation to herself, imagining she could feel the heated flesh of his cock throughout the length of her channel. Her pleasure shot upwards as she focused upon the sensations his turgid flesh produced as it stroked her.

Through the palms she stroked along his big body, she felt a quaking begin inside him as he neared his crisis. Her body responded, shooting upward higher, toward the brink, hovering at the edge. His cock jerked as he reached his peak and she felt his hot seed begin to spill into her channel. The convulsions of his rapture pushed her over the precipice into explosive ecstasy that was so intense that when she descended, she fell into absolute darkness.

Chapter Ten

Ja-rael rested as much of his weight on his arms and thighs as he could, struggling to catch his breath. It took a tremendous effort even to support himself that much, for he felt completely drained, but he was afraid his weight would crush Leez if he didn't. When he could breathe more freely, he leaned down to stroke his face along hers, scarcely conscious of the love words he murmured to her in his own tongue. She stirred, halfheartedly returning his caresses before she drifted away.

Sighing with a mixture of resignation and relief, Ja-rael gathered her to him and rolled onto his side, propping on one arm to study her sleeping face while he waited for his body to relax enough that he could separate himself from her. It had long been the custom of his people to use the time after mating to express their appreciation of and affection for their mate. It was a time of closeness without passion to enjoy being united, being as one. He could scarcely quibble, he supposed, when he'd done his utmost to thoroughly exhaust her--and it was a relief at least not to have her snipping at him for something he could not help-- but he still could not prevent the sense of being used and dismissed from clouding his pleasure.

Doubts crowded close and he couldn't help but wonder if there had been anything rational about his decision to keep Leez anyway--in spite of the nearly insurmountable odds he now saw against their ever finding peace between them. He found, however, that the longer he studied her sleeping face, the more certain he was that he could not have made any other decision.

She was going to be furious when she realized what he'd done.

Doubt shook him again at that thought, but this time he dismissed it. Moving away from her as his body finally returned to normal, he dressed quickly and quietly, then stepped from the cabin and secured the door, bending the latch and barricading it to make certain she could not escape again.

He went down into the hold then, studying the creatures he'd pinned his future upon--the mate price. Lioness or not, she was worth every one and more. Finally, he decided only to take half, however, realizing he had not planned as well as he'd originally thought. He would need to provide for her and make her comfortable and he didn't want to have to wait until he traded again to do so. He would leave half for her family and a note explaining that he would bring more on his next trip. The other half he would take with him to insure Leez's comfort and well being.

He couldn't recall seeing a pen for animals, so he gathered up rope and, after a good deal of aggravation, managed to secure the creatures he meant to take to her family and disembarked with them. It was still dark when he arrived at the habitat. After looking around for a likely spot to leave the livestock, he finally tied them along a length of post, brought them water and then, after he'd secured the note he'd written within sight of the main entrance, headed back to the ship.

He'd lingered longer than he'd intended to on Torrine and he was anxious to get home.

* * * *

Awareness came to Elise slowly. She didn't particularly welcome it. She felt so wonderfully relaxed and satisfied all she really wanted to do was to curl up and drift deeply asleep once more.

She'd almost dropped off the edge when something began to tease at the back of her mind, some vague sense of wrongness.

The mattress beneath her was wrong.

The darkness surrounding her was wrong.

And the scent that lingered in the sheets wasn't her own-- not altogether.

Struggling upright, she tried to focus her eyes.

The cabin looked like the inside of a cave and still she knew it wasn't her cabin. She always had some light, even if it was no more than the glow of a clock or night light because she frequently woke at night and it unnerved and disoriented her to find herself in pitch black darkness.

It was possible the lights had gone out, but she didn't think that was it at all. The cabin simply didn't 'feel' right.

Finally, she was roused enough she decided to investigate. Feeling around for the edge of the bed, she climbed out and, waving her hands in front of her, staggered a little drunkenly toward the faint glow that indicated a porthole. It was almost as dark outside as it was in the cabin. Undoubtedly the moon, which was so tiny it shed very little light anyway, had set.

After trying to penetrate the gloom for several moments, she finally decided that she was simply too disoriented with sleep to figure it out. Feeling her way back, she climbed onto the mattress, curled on her side and drifted off again.

She woke up when she felt the pallet vibrating beneath her.

For several moments, she couldn't figure out what was happening. There was absolutely no doubt in her mind when the ship left the ground, however.

The G's the thing was pulling plastered her to the pallet for what seemed an eternity. Abruptly, it ceased. She'd already begun floating toward the ceiling of the cabin when the artificial gravity kicked in. She hit the pallet and bounced off of it. Fortunately, the mattress absorbed most of the concussion of the fall, but she managed to bite her tongue.

She was still wondering how she'd managed to catch her tongue between her teeth when the door opened.

"Did you fall?"

Elise gave Ja-rael a drop dead look. "There's a very good reason they make take-off harnesses," she growled, getting to her feet with an effort.

"The ship only has one seat," he said uncomfortably.

"Which means it should only be carrying *one* person! I can't believe you took off with me still here!" She braked the moment the words left her mouth. "Wait a minute! *How* did I get here? *Why* am I here?"

Ja-rael looked uncomfortable. "You do not remember?"

Elise's eyes narrowed, but not altogether because she was struggling to remember. She knew he wouldn't be looking guilty if he hadn't done something. After some prodding, her mind finally began to yield up snippets of memory. As the dots connected, Elise felt anger take hold. "You did it on purpose!" she said accusingly.

"What?" he asked evasively.

"Don't you even *try* to act innocent! You *know* I'm not in my right mind when you hit me with your super charged pheromones. And I distinctly remember you insisting on coming back to the ship. You did it on purpose!"

His gaze slid away. "I feel desire or not. I can not make it happen."

"Maybe not, but you knew exactly what you were doing when you held out until we got back to the ship."

"I did."

If possible, Elise was more outraged by the admission than the denial before. She gasped at his audacity.

"You had already agreed to be my mate."

"I did no...." Elise broke off. "I was under the influence," she ended testily, "and you damned well knew it!"

"All the same."

"It's not all the same, damn it!"

His eyes narrowed. "I asked more than once. Each time you insisted. You said ...."

Elise held up a hand to stop him. "Don't tell me what I said. I don't even want to remember what I said, and certainly not what I did." She thought it over. "And I suppose that ... that marathon last night just happened?"

He studied her for several moments, his own anger aroused at last. "No. I knew you would change your mind the moment you'd had what you wanted."

Elise gasped at him in outrage. "Don't you dare try to make me the bad guy! I was completely honest with you."

He held up one finger. "One cycle. If you still wish to be free, I will return you to your people."

Elise blinked. "Is that supposed to be a negotiation?"

His lips tightened. "By both Tor and Meeri law, we are bound. We have mated--thoroughly. I know that it was wrong to steal you away, but you were willing to mate. You can not deny that. I did not force you to accept me. I do not have to offer to release you. The laws will support my claim. But I want ...." He stopped abruptly, leaving the rest of the sentence hanging. "If you will agree to try to learn acceptance, then I will agree that if you can not, I will return you to your people and set you free."

Elise studied him, trying to think calmly. The truth was, she really wasn't in any position to negotiate. She would've rather had her fingernails pulled out than to have to admit that she'd not only been perfectly willing, she'd practically raped him--not that she could help it--but she couldn't lie to herself no matter how badly she wanted to. Beyond that, he'd taken off and she didn't have a clue of how to pilot any ship, let alone this thing that hardly deserved the name.

She wasn't going to get back on her own steam.

It was possible that she might be able to persuade someone on Meeri to take her back, but that was a long shot and she had a bad feeling that Ja-rael wasn't lying about the laws.

"Exactly how long is one cycle?" she asked suspiciously.

"The circuit of the world around the sun."

"A year!" Elise exclaimed, outraged. "A *year*!"

He drew in a long suffering breath. "There is only one-- very brief--time a year that the worlds of Tor and Meeri are close enough for the trip."

He didn't look like he was lying. There was also the fact that she'd never seen a Meeri on Tor before, which seemed to support his claim.

Lifting the robe to keep from tripping over the hem, she stalked to the pallet and sat down. A year--a year by the cycle of the Meeri world, which could be anything. They were still counting days by the Earth calendar.

"I don't understand the Meeri customs, but what I do understand, I don't like," she said sullenly. "I could never fit in."

He crossed the room and knelt in front of her. "You are intelligent. You can if you try."

"You don't understand at all."

"I will try."

"I don't *want* to fit in! I don't want to be like those women I've seen in the market in the Torrine city, swathed in veils, guarded like a bird in a cage! I'm a person! I'm used to being treated like one--not a--thing that some man owns, damn it!"

His lips tightened. "I am Meeri, not Torrine. We are not like them. How can you judge when you do not even know us?"

Elise couldn't prevent the blush that rose in her cheeks, but she was a long way from being convinced. She didn't know why he was even trying to convince her. It wasn't like she had a choice.

Finally, she nodded.

Looking surprisingly relieved all things considered, he smiled and her stomach performed a little jitter dance. He had a very nice smile. He was so handsome already it was hard to see how the simple act of smiling could make him more so, but so it was.

"Are you hungry?"

She was always hungry. She'd been hungry since she woke from the hyber unit.

He chuckled at the hopeful look that crossed her face, took her hand and helped her to her feet. When she was standing, he looked her over. "This looks better on you than it does on me."

Elise was embarrassed and not just for appropriating something that didn't belong to her. She'd ripped it escaping and soiled it when she'd sprawled in the dirt--and then soaked it in the stream--and finally slept in it, much of the night anyway. "Sorry. I didn't have anything to wear."

"When we reach Meeri, I will take you to the market and you may choose whatever you like."

She had mixed feelings about that, but she kept her thoughts to herself. She was far more interested in the food.

It looked as if Ja-rael had modified the forward cabin to squeeze in a tiny 'mess', which explained why there was only one seat--the pilot's seat. She wondered what the rear cabin, now captain's cabin, had been before he'd remodeled the ship. The table was about two foot square--not much room even for one. She bumped her knee when she seated herself in the only dining chair.

Wincing, she rubbed it until the pain passed, wondering how Ja-rael, who was a good bit larger than she, managed to get around the cramped ship without beating himself to death. He must be very well coordinated.

Almost the moment the thought flitted through her mind, he banged his head on something jutting from the ceiling as he removed a container from the cooling unit and straightened. Elise bit her lip, fighting the inappropriate amusement that went through her as he rubbed his head and checked his hand for blood.

"Are you all right?" she asked sympathetically.

He glanced at her in surprise, an expression of embarrassment flickering across his face. Finally, he merely nodded and returned his attention to the food he was heating in the heating unit.

Elise's stomach growled as the smell wafted in her direction. He smiled faintly as he set the container of food before her and turned away again to draw a container of water.

"You're not eating?" she asked when he'd set that on the table as well and stepped back.

"There is only one of each. I can wait."

So he wasn't in the habit of entertaining while he was on these trips. Feeling a little uncomfortable, Elise picked up the utensil he handed her and tested the food. Whatever it was it was either very good or she was so hungry anything would've tasted like ambrosia to her. To her relief, she saw when she glanced up that he'd moved away and settled in the control seat.

Curiosity finally overcame her sense of discomfort as she ate. She glanced at him several times, wondering about him in particular, but also about the strange mixture of technology and what she at least considered archaic customs of the civilization he was taking her to.

"Have you been trading long?"

He seemed to think it over. "I have come three times."

She looked at him in surprise, then realized that she had no idea of his age. Not that it mattered, she supposed. It was a relative thing. If every world determined a year by the revolution of their world around its sun, then no two had the same length of year. Tor's, as near as they could tell, was longer than Earth's by nearly a month. Meeri would almost certainly be further out--Tor was so hot it was hard to believe anyone could survive on a world closer to the sun--which would make its year longer still.

She didn't want to think about that, though.

"You said you were a healer. Why do you trade? I mean, is everybody that healthy on Meeri?"

He looked uncomfortable. "The poor are less healthy because of the hardships of their lives. They are as willing to pay, but often not able to pay much or even any for care. The wealthy can pay, but they are more likely to be healthy because they live well. I lived well enough." He stopped, frowning. "I began to trap and trade to fill the time."

She stared at him for several moments, digesting what he'd said. Finally, she realized he was saying he'd been lonely--or at least bored with the time he had on his hands between treating patients.

It wasn't something she'd experienced much of since they'd landed on Tor. She hadn't had the chance to experience much boredom in the last few years she'd spent on Earth, for that matter, but she remembered what it was like--the sense of restlessness, the vague 'ache' that seemed in need of filling and the search for something to fill it. In general, one didn't even know what one needed. There was just a restless quest to find that nebulous something.

She stopped eating this time before she hurt herself. Thanking him, she was on the point of retreating to the cabin once more when it occurred to her that she'd given him her word that she would make an attempt to come to terms with the situation. She didn't think there was any possibility of it, but she didn't like to go back on her word, even if she'd been forced by circumstances to give it. Besides, she couldn't work on getting him to accept the futility of his plans if she spent her time in hiding.

Beyond that, she was scared to death. She needed to assure herself that she had no real reason to be afraid--or find out if she did have a reason to be afraid.

Instead of returning to the cabin, she settled in the chair he vacated and studied her hands thoughtfully. "On your world, does it take many years of study to become a healer?"

He nodded. "I began on my fifteenth anniversary."

Elise's brows rose in surprise. "That young? How many years did you study?"

"I study still."

She frowned. "How many years did you study before you began to practice?"

"Six."

"And how many years have you been practicing?" she asked tentatively.

He threw her a laughing look. "I am in my prime."

She couldn't help it, she smiled back. "That doesn't tell me anything."

He looked puzzled. "Prime breeding years."

Elise frowned and finally shrugged. "That still doesn't tell me anything. It could be the same years as it is for us, or not. The human male can produce--well, virtually their entire life. Their sexual peak is around the age of eighteen, but I've never been entirely sure if that meant 'prowess' or 'production'. Since I'm not a man, I never was interested enough to find out."

He frowned, pushing his food away. "You think there is so much difference between us?"

"How can you be a physician and *not* notice? You're not seeing it either because you don't want to, or maybe because you're seeing what you expect to see."

He looked away from her. "It is only small things."

"It's more than small things, and you know as well as I do that we're talking external. On a molecular level the difference could be vast."

He grew angry. "There is a point to this?"

Elise simply stared at him for several moments, wondering why she'd taken the conversation down this road. She hadn't intended to provoke another argument. She'd just wanted to know more about him. Still, she found her own anger rising to match his. "Maybe I'm scared. I'm sure it never occurred to you to consider anything from my perspective, but from where I'm sitting things are looking pretty damned scary all the way around. It would be bad enough to be taken away by a stranger of my own species, but at least I'd have some idea of what to expect. You're not only a stranger, you're of a different culture, a different world, a different species so far as I can tell. And we're mating here. Yes, I know I seemed willing, but that's because I was drugged, intentionally or not, and not able to form a rational decision. What if ... what if I should become impregnated? What if we aren't compatible, that way, at all? And, even if we are and everything goes just right, what if I hate your world, and your culture and want to go home?"

She got to her feet abruptly. "Maybe I'm thinking it would've been nice if you'd spent a little more time thinking about how I'd feel about all of this instead of behaving like a … just like a typical self-centered human being!"

Chapter Eleven

Elise realized the moment she stalked off toward the cabin that she didn't feel one iota better having spoken her mind and expressed her concerns. Shouldn't she feel better, having gotten it off her chest?

Slamming the cabin door behind her, she stomped to the bed and flopped down on it to sulk.

It occurred to her fairly quickly that she'd been so agitated she'd railed at Ja-rael in English, a language he had no grasp of whatsoever, throwing in a word or two of Torrine now and then just to add to the confusion. No wonder he'd only stared at her blankly when she went off on him.

That wasn't the real reason she didn't feel any better, though, she realized finally. She didn't feel one bit better because she felt bad for feeling the way she did when Ja-rael had done nothing at all, really, to make her feel threatened. She felt guilty, as if she were in the wrong-- because she was blaming him when she knew she shouldn't.

The situation wasn't one where culpability could easily and comfortably be placed on someone else. She knew that she was at least partly responsible for it. She couldn't blame Ja-rael for something he really had no control over. It wasn't his fault his pheromones had such an effect on her-- she had a feeling he was as stunned and disconcerted by it as she was--and while she was being honest, her own lack of self-control bothered her a lot.

Nervous--worried--she decided that would've been a better way to express her concerns. She wasn't afraid of Ja-rael, or his people for that matter, and she knew the chances were at least fifty/fifty that the living conditions were no worse than what she had to endure here and most likely at least somewhat better since they were well established on their world.

After mulling the situation over in her mind for a good two hours, she finally pinpointed the real source of her anxiety. She was afraid of the entire 'family' thing, worried she would be found lacking. She didn't remember a lot about what had happened and what had been said the night before, but she recalled more than she was comfortable with.

Ja-rael had decided to take her with him because he felt committed already because they'd had sex. He was disappointed to discover she wasn't what he'd thought she was, a maned lioness, and worried she couldn't give him a family, but he felt obligated to take her anyway because of his laws and customs.

It would've been so much easier if she just hadn't known that part. As long as he was worshipping at her feet and she'd known, but he hadn't, that she wasn't the same species, she'd been able to feel superior about being human. Now, in the blink of an eye, she'd been relegated to inferior goods and an obligation.

Before, he'd not only thought she was beautiful, he'd been proud of the fact that he'd gotten such a beautiful and rare mate. Now, he was probably embarrassed about his mistake and embarrassed about being stuck with her.

She felt like crying.

It made her angry. It wasn't as if it was *her* fault she wasn't a maned lioness!

She would be willing to bet it was going to turn out to be her fault, too, if it transpired that she couldn't be bred.

That part, she realized, scared the hell out of her. She'd come from a society that had had rigid birth control for generations. Strict breeding regulations had been implemented when the world population had spiraled completely out of control. The devastation that had followed had only made birth control more critical because food and medicines and even places to live had become harder and harder to come by. Not even the exodus from the dying solar system had changed that, for resources only became more limited.

They had arrived on Tor with only enough to provide for those onboard for two years--rationed--which would give them a fighting chance to establish a productive colony. If they'd immediately begun reproducing, every addition to the colony would have narrowed their margin of safety in that regard. She didn't even know if she could produce a healthy child under ideal conditions. Cross breeding, if it was possible, might actually produce a stronger, healthier child than one that was 'pure' human, since humans had over bred to the point that they were passing on more undesirable attributes than desirable ones, but that was assuming it would work at all.

Elise's mental debate came to a screeching halt there as it suddenly dawned on her to wonder why she was worried about that at all. She didn't actually *want* things to work out, did she? She was only going along with all this because she didn't have a choice, wasn't she?

Why should she be worried about whether Ja-rael was proud, or ashamed, of her? Whether she could give him the family he wanted or not? She was just going to stay as long as she had to and go back to her own people, wasn't she?

Agitated by her thoughts, she got up and left the cabin, but she discovered that it was easier to leave the room than to leave the worrisome thoughts behind.

Ja-rael glanced at her, but immediately returned his attention to the view from the forward viewing screen. After standing uncomfortably for several moments, Elise looked around for a place to sit. There wasn't one, of course, except the seat she'd vacated shortly before at the table.

After staring at the back of his head for a good ten minutes, Elise finally nerved herself to offer an olive branch. "I should … uh … I would *like* to learn to speak in your tongue."

Ja-rael turned to study her speculatively for several moments and she almost felt as if she could read what was going through his mind, but perhaps that was just her guilty conscience? He had every reason to be suspicious of her motives. Finally, he nodded, after studying it over frowningly for several moments, he got up and began to search the ship for something, finally unearthing a rectangular object. Tucking it under his arm, he looked around for a spot to settle and finally gestured toward the cabin.

Curious, Elise followed him, settling a little uneasily beside him on the bunk. She saw then that the object was some sort of electronic writing tablet.

"You will need to know how to read and write the language as well as speak it," he said without glancing at her.

Elise studied the strange symbols uneasily. She'd been thinking more along the lines of learning a few phrases, or a fairly large vocabulary that she could throw out in combination with hand gestures. She relaxed slightly, however, when she discovered that the language of the Meeri, like the romance languages of Old Earth, was based on the same root language as the one spoken by the Torrines. Most of the words were only pronounced a little differently and she'd already learned a fair grasp of that, although she certainly hadn't learned to read or write the language.

Settling more comfortably on the side of the bunk, she worked on memorizing the way each letter and word looked and sounding them out. In the process, her discomfort vanished and she began to interact more freely with Ja-rael.

"Good," he said after a while, tapping her cheek affectionately. "You learn quickly."

Pleased with the praise, Elise smiled at him. "I can teach you my language, too," she offered.

He smiled back, but wryly. "I grasp much," he responded in English. "When you are angry, I am asshole. Same thing your people, because not come to look for you."

Elise felt her jaw go slack with surprise. "You understand ...."

"Much. I see your face, I understand what you feel. Help to understand what you say." He got up. "Study. I do not want my people to think you are a savage," he said in Torrine.

When he'd gone, Elise collapsed back against the mattress and covered her face in embarrassment, frantically trying to figure out everything that had been said around him that he might, or might not, have understood.

Her tirade earlier?

Probably the gist of it anyway, maybe more than just a general idea.

The remark about the 'savage' certainly seemed to indicate that he'd understood a good bit of the conversation in the habitat. How? Had he *absorbed* it?

How the hell was she supposed to know he would pick up her language with such ease?

Maybe she should have reserved judgment until she'd gotten to know him a little better?

So, she wasn't *as* guilty of snobbery as the others, but she had a feeling she'd been just a little condescending because he'd made a mistake she thought he could've figured out if he'd been more intelligent. But people tended to see what they expected to see, or interpret what they saw by what was known to them, so it was no wonder he'd mistaken her for his kind. He obviously hadn't been expecting to run into aliens. She, on the other hand, had known she was living among aliens.

So, maybe, they'd both made an honest mistake and neither of them should be so quick to judge?

Regardless of her own sense of guilt, it took Elise the better part of two days to get over the bulk of her anger over being tricked and shanghaied. It might have taken longer except for the fact that it was slowly born in upon her that Ja-rael wasn't any happier about the fact that she wasn't what he'd thought than she had been at the prospect of being wooed by an alien. She began to get a bad feeling she'd fallen right off the pedestal he'd put her on into a hell of a gully. That upset her far more than it should have considering her own feelings on the matter. Even worse to her way of thinking, she came to realize that she hadn't felt his desire *once* since they'd taken off, not even distant vibes. It was disturbing how distressing that was.

It was even more disturbing to realize she'd not only accused him of using it against her, she'd excused herself by blaming him--because she was pretty sure he'd understood and maybe that was why she wasn't feeling that magical glow.

Of course, it hadn't even been twenty four hours since they'd had sex--and it had been a marathon--so maybe he just wasn't in the mood because he was sated for the time being?

She didn't feel particularly needy.

She just wanted a little reassurance.

She didn't get it. Two more days passed and he didn't even show a flicker of interest and she was beginning to feel a little needy.

The cruiser didn't just look old, it acted antiquated--slow. When she finally asked how long the trip would take she was dismayed when he told her--almost two weeks Old Earth time--she still calculated everything in Old Earth time. She didn't know why she persisted in clinging to it, but no other measurements seemed 'right'.

As tiny as the cruiser was, it was impossible to put any sort of distance between them, physically or emotionally. She spent most of her time in the cabin, because it was the only area that actually had enough room to move around without bumping into anything. Ja-rael spent as little time there as possible, making it a point to rest when she was up and moving around.

Elise was finally forced to conclude that he'd not only gotten a firm grasp of her tirade, the remarks so closely mirrored his own concerns that he was trying to avoid thinking about them by avoiding her--which was no easy task on such a small vessel.

It probably hadn't helped that she'd said she was afraid of him.

She wasn't, not really. She'd laid into him pretty hard several times in their short acquaintance and hardly even managed to arouse a spark of anger. He was so 'laid back' if not for the aggressive way he'd behaved at the habitat she would've been more inclined to think he was incapable of being aroused to real anger, much less violence and she simply couldn't imagine him being any sort of threat to her under the circumstances. More accurately, she was just plain afraid of the 'unknown' that awaited her.

Ja-rael had said that he would protect her. She didn't doubt his willingness, or even his ability to keep her safe from most any harm that might befall, but there were just some things one couldn't be protected from.

What if she made a complete fool out of herself because she didn't know or understand some really important custom? What if she unwittingly broke some law? Insulted someone important?

What if she didn't have to actually do anything wrong? What if she was just ostracized because she wasn't like everyone else?

Some of her fears might sound just plain silly voiced aloud, but they weren't 'nothing'. They weren't groundless, or unimportant. Life as a pariah could be pure hell, even if hell only lasted one year.

And how long *was* one year on Meeri?

Chapter Twelve

Five days into the trip from Tor to Meeri Elise had reached a point of distress that made one 'truth' impossible to ignore or give the lie to. She was addicted to the chemical reaction Ja-rael's pheromones created when they bombarded her body. She did her best to control it, ignore it, beat the craving into submission, but from the time she woke until the time she finally managed to fall asleep during the rest periods she had a hard time thinking about anything else. It wouldn't have been so bad if Ja-rael had seemed to be suffering equally from an addiction to her. She could have at least consoled herself with the thought that he really wanted her, even though he was too hurt, angry, or maybe disgusted about the situation to try to bed her. She wasn't even certain of that much, however.

He was polite. She supposed one could even say friendly, in a standoffish sort of way. He would sit companionably with her for hours, teaching her about Meeri, the language, customs, history--He was even willing to share an occasional anecdote about himself, but she almost felt as if he'd erected an invisible wall between them. Occasionally, she would feel a faint wave of interest, but she'd hardly registered it before it disappeared and left her wondering whether she'd actually felt it or if she just wanted to feel it so much that she was beginning to imagine it.

When she managed to convince herself she hadn't imagined the sensation, she was irritated. She saw no reason not to enjoy themselves. Assuming the prolonged hyber-sleep hadn't affected it--which it shouldn't have--by her calculations, her birth control devise had a good five years life left to it. Unless she deliberately disabled it, the chances of finding out whether they were, or were not, compatible breeders wasn't an issue, but, somehow, she had a feeling that Ja-rael wouldn't particularly welcome that news, particularly since the realization that there might be a problem seemed to have completely turned him off to the idea of having sex with her at all.

* * * *

There was nothing to see beyond the forward viewing port that had not been there every day since they'd taken off. Regardless, Ja-rael focused upon it almost with a sense of desperation, and still he was aware of every move Elise made in the cramped confines of his ship.

Under the circumstances, it should not have been difficult for him to control his desires. It should not have been difficult under *any* circumstances. He had had a lifetime of learning self control in an environment where it was extremely hazardous to one's health to lust for a female that belonged to another male and even more dangerous to lust for an unmated female. Why was he having such a hard time controlling his hunger for a female that was not even his kind?

The sense of betrayal he felt was almost equal to his embarrassment for making such a horrendous mistake.

Why had it not occurred to him, even once, that she might be a member of the alien race that he had heard had settled on Tor? It wasn't as if his desire had so consumed him that he hadn't noticed there were differences between them.

And yet he had put it all down to some absurd legend that he had never even truly believed--before he'd set eyes on Elise. He hadn't thought that he had placed any credence in the stories he'd heard in his childhood. Perhaps he had though? Maybe, deep down, even though he'd thought education and maturity had eradicated childish fantasies, maybe they never truly were. Perhaps they always remained, only awaiting a spark to come to life again?

Or, perhaps, it was just Elise?

Why? He supposed that question bothered him the most. Why had he been so consumed by his desire for her the moment he saw her that he had acted only upon his instincts as if his brain had completely shut down and ceased to function at all?

By all that he knew about his physiology, he should not have even felt any attraction at all if they were so completely different. Hostility would have been a more natural reaction. At the very least, he should have felt some sense of 'wrongness'. She was an intelligent being, so his feelings could not be considered unnatural in the sense that he was desirous of mating with a lower order of animal, but even so he found it confusing and disturbing.

Her people had looked upon him as if he were a dumb beast. He had sensed their belief in their superiority even before he had begun to understand their words.

Elise also felt that her race was far superior to his own.

He had sensed that almost from the beginning in the way she had behaved toward him afterward. He had not been insulted then. He had felt that he was a humble supplicant to a far superior being--for the legends of the maned lions equated them almost with gods. When he had finally been forced to accept that he had behaved like a complete fool anger had supplanted his sense of humility. He was not inferior. His people were not inferior to these strange folk from a distant star.

The problem was worsened by the fact that he had committed himself in those moments of insanity. Whatever his misunderstanding of the situation, he was bound now by his own laws, traditions, and even more insurmountable, his psyche. He could not unbind himself. He could have left her. He had wanted to. He had wanted to flee from his humiliation and hide it both from himself and his peers, but his desires had been at war the moment the thought had occurred to him. He didn't know if he could live without the female he had chosen for his mate, but he knew he didn't want to try. He could not face the emptiness he knew would hound him forever. He would not be able to take another mate to ease his suffering. He would be alone. Forever.

Taking her with him was almost worse. His hunger for her was beginning to erode every attempt at reason and control. Despite her body's reaction to him, on an intellectual level she was repulsed by him, seemed to find most everything about him repugnant, most notably his body's tendency to seal his seed inside her once they'd mated--which was obviously something totally alien to her. That knowledge made self control a little easier, but only a little. He was rapidly reaching the point where he was beyond caring how she felt about it afterwards.

What bothered him most about the entire situation beyond his immediate needs was the realization that his line would end with him because of the lack of reason he had shown in choosing his mate. He knew it was likely that she was right and their races were probably incompatible for reproduction. It was almost as horrifying to think they might succeed and produce something pathetically defective as it was frustrating to realize the family he had envisioned for himself was unlikely to materialize.

It was all the more disheartening because he had been thinking, when he was able to think rationally about Elise at all, that she was a creature of such perfection that they could not help but produce physically and mentally superior offspring that would have been a source of both pride and joy to him. With that thought, he glanced toward Elise. He was almost immediately sorry he had.

She was cleaning the cooking area. The movement of her body as she wiped the table with a damp cloth caused her breasts to sway in a motion that was instantly mesmerizing. His gaze zeroed in on the undulating motion of the soft globes and his mind followed. They were soft, white and the tips puckered and erect as if a lover had caressed them. Heat immediately followed that thought and before he realized it his body responded with the blinding swiftness of arousal of more than a week of deprivation of the honeyed ecstasy he had become addicted to from the first moment of mating.

* * * *

Elise put the first flash of heat down to her labors. Boredom had driven her to find *some* outlet for her frustration even though the galley was hardly in need of cleaning. The warmth was followed almost immediately by the internal chemical scent she recognized and directly behind that a wave of weakness and dizziness. She didn't dare look up for fear it would break whatever spell had captured Ja-rael's interest and allow him to withdraw again, but she wasn't sure of what she'd done to entice him in the first place. She hadn't taken any particular pains with her appearance. She was wearing what she had since they'd left Tor, yet another of his robes which were virtually identical in every way.

Was it the domesticity of the situation, then?

Ignoring the growing debilitation of the drug her body produced in response to his desire, she continued what she was doing and finally nerved herself to take a quick peek at him. His eyes were glazed and focused on her breasts.

A shiver of responding desire went through her, but also a touch of surprise and behind that pleasure and a touch of amusement.

He was as fascinated by the female breasts as the vast majority of Earth males.

Her heart kicked into high gear, pumping the drug of desire through her more rapidly, sending waves of heat crashing through her that made her flesh prickle with anticipated sensations.

He shot to his feet abruptly and Elise paused in her task to look up at him quickly.

Her heart failed her when she saw the struggle he was waging with himself. She knew the very moment he shifted from intent to escape. The realization prompted her own war. She never consciously made a decision. She simply stepped back to block his path as he moved to stalk past her. They collided none too gently and he grabbed her instinctively to keep her from falling. His touch seared her, burning away the dregs of reason that remained to her.

Apparently, it had the same effect upon him. He'd no more than set her away from him than he jerked her back so that she was plastered full length against him. His scent, the heat of his body, the feel of his flesh sent a firestorm through her. Her arms were pinioned by his grip, preventing her from running her hands over him. Instead, she rubbed her cheek along his hard chest, nuzzling him. Uttering a sound much like a growl, he snatched her off her feet.

The confines of the ship made it impossible for him to carry her in his arms. The moment he realized it, he shifted her, tossing her over his shoulder. She landed with a grunt as the air was pushed from her lungs, but ignored the discomfort in her pursuit of gathering him into her senses by running her palms along the hard muscles of his back. The gratification was only momentary. She'd barely begun her exploration when her world tilted once more as he dropped her onto the bed.

Her body felt as if it was on fire with fever by that time. The coolness of the sheets as she touched down was almost painful, far more uncomfortable than the landing itself on the soft, yielding surface. Her skin instantly erupted into stinging goose bumps. The heat of his body as he settled on her mellowed the sensation, then altered it into acute pleasure. She wrestled with his weight to open her body to him, eager to join at once. He settled between her thighs when she spread them for him, but seemed in no great hurry to bury his cock in her. Impatience threaded her desire. She moved against him, rubbing her clit along the hard ridge of his erection.

Ignoring the demand for immediate gratification, he lifted slightly away from her, pressing her down into the mattress with his hands when she surged upward. Before she could protest with more than a soft sound of distress, he dipped his head and covered her mouth with his own. Elise responded hungrily, making love to his mouth with her tongue and coaxing him to do the same. When he did, exploring the sensitive inner surfaces of her mouth with the faint roughness of his tongue, flooding her with his essence, her body erupted into a tiny quake of release. Closing her mouth around his tongue, she sucked it greedily as the waves of delightful sensation jolted through her.

He groaned in reaction, his great body shaking with the effort to retain his control. Finally, he tore his mouth free of hers, gasping for air as he shifted lower, exploring her throat and breasts with his mouth and tongue. Elise moaned, feeling her body respond instantly to the lure of more--more pleasure, more sensation--exquisite tension.

By the time he shifted and buried the head of his cock in her opening, Elise had begun to demand his possession-- in Meeri, in English-- in Torrine when he seemed to ignore the other commands. She bit down on his shoulder to contain a scream of delight when he began to plow his way past resisting flesh, plunging and retreating in short sorties to gain possession of agonizing inches of wonderfully receptive nerves and flesh. She came again as he finally filled her completely, basking in the electric sizzle of release through tightly wound muscles. It seemed to go on forever as he began to stroke his cock in and out of her passage, quakes that reached a zenith and stayed there for an almost agonizing length of time before the wave broke crest and she began to descend. His rhythm caught her once more before she hit bottom, lifting her again.

Digging her heels into the soft mattress, she countered each thrust, urging him to find a rhythm that would take her to the peak once more. He made a sound that was part desire, part frustration as he tried to hold his own pleasure to him a little longer. She stroked him almost apologetically, knowing he would have his pleasure only once, but too caught up in her own body's demand for release to refrain from responding to her enjoyment of being possessed by him, his heady scent, the delight of touching his big, supple body.

Her caresses pushed him beyond his control. She felt a tremor flow through him, felt his cock jerk in the first spasms of his culmination. The realization that she'd brought him to release sent her over the edge for the third time. It was harder, more intense than the first two, nearly tearing consciousness from her grasp. In a blissful haze of gratitude, she stroked him lazily when he collapsed on top of her at last, enjoying his weight upon her. He responded by caressing her in a way that spoke of a lover's appreciation, nuzzling her neck, tracing a necklace of light kisses along her collarbone and throat. Moments passed before she realized that the words he was murmuring were love words.

Chapter Thirteen

Elise wasn't aware of giving her sudden understanding away, but evidently she did. Ja-rael ceased to speak, leaving her clutching at the few words she'd managed to decipher and struggling to string them together. She gave up the effort when he shifted, moving away from her to lie beside her on the bed, more interested in prolonging the moments of intimacy and harmony between them than interpreting what she knew must be the meaningless little nothings of a lover.

As he settled beside her, she rolled onto her side and slipped an arm around him, snuggling close. He stiffened, but after a moment relaxed fractionally, stroking her hair as if he couldn't resist touching it. Finally, he sighed gustily. "We should not do this. We are playing a dangerous game with the life of an innocent."

It took Elise several moments to figure out he was referring to the possibility of impregnating her. She chuckled. "We're not. I have birth control."

He pulled away and stared down at her. "You have what?"

Elise studied him uncomfortably. She sensed that it was more than puzzlement that caused the new tension in him. "I can keep from getting pregnant."

There was no doubt in her mind then that he wasn't particularly pleased with that information. Disbelief, revulsion and, she suspected, a touch of contempt chased across his features. "Your people can do this?"

Shivering at the sudden chill in his voice, she pulled away and sat up, looking around for the robe she'd discarded. "Yours can't?" she countered, making no effort to keep the trace of cool superiority out of her voice.

"Why?" he asked instead of answering her question.

"Why what?"

He slid off the bed and snatched his loincloth from the floor, donning it with angry, jerky movements. "Why would you want to be able to control it?"

"Overpopulation? Indiscriminate breeding?" she said tartly. "Then, too, it evens the playing field so that women can enjoy themselves as much as men without the unpleasant consequences."

"Unpleasant consequences? Off spring, you mean?"

Elise glared at him. "Now why, I wonder, did I think this would be something you would understand only because you're a male of another species? Primitive man was the same way! Thinking pleasure in intercourse was something they alone should experience--which, by the way is not only completely unfair, but downright stupid! Why would a woman want to if she isn't getting anything out of it?"

His lips tightened. "For the joy of offspring?"

Elise gaped at him for several moments in stunned disbelief and outrage. "Give me a break! The joy of how damned many? The women of my species can bear young for twenty or thirty years. In ancient times, before we learned to control pregnancies, women often had ten or fifteen, and sometimes, with multiple births, twenty or thirty or even more. Just how much damned joy do you think a woman can take?"

He stared at her blankly, his expression patently disbelieving. "This is not possible."

"This *is* possible--for us, anyway! They teach us this in sex classes when we're young so that we'll understand the importance of birth control, because it was the indiscriminate breeding of earlier generations that got us into so much trouble to begin with. When one man and one woman produced so many, do you have any idea of the pyramid that would create in only two or three more generations---all genetically connected and subject to passing on undesirable or downright deadly genetic traits?"

He frowned. "I saw nothing to indicate your people are not strong and healthy."

"They are now because we finally reached a point in our technology to not only control births, but to eliminate genetic diseases and susceptibilities to diseases. A lot of people suffered and died that didn't have to before that. And the truly awful thing is, we've almost come full cycle and are right back where we started--except that now we know what can happen if we aren't careful. We just can't do a damn thing about it because we've lost so much of our technology."

He still looked skeptical, but at that he swallowed a little sickly and departed.

Elise stared at the door as it closed behind him, feeling her anger slowly fade and a sense of defeat take its place. She'd routed him. She supposed she'd won the argument in a sense, but it wasn't the victory she'd wanted. How had things gone so wrong, she wondered with sudden irritation? She'd started out trying to convince him there was no reason why they couldn't enjoy themselves and ended up convincing him that … What?

She had the uncomfortable conviction that both she and the race she hailed from had come off as being less than desirable morally and ethically. She resented the feeling, knowing it was more a matter of having expressed herself badly. Or perhaps it was only the reflection of his assessment against his own customs and beliefs that made her feel somehow inferior.

That thought irritated her. His stupid customs weren't her problem. It wasn't her fault that she was human and not like his people. Obviously, birth control wasn't something the Meeri worried about, or perhaps not something they had to worry about, though she was damned if she could figure out the why or how of that. Maybe the females just weren't capable of bearing young for very long? Or maybe they weren't very fertile?

It could be anything, up to and including a population so low, and so torn by disease and poor living conditions that life expectancy was low anyway.

It wasn't a comforting thought, but it at least made her feel better about the fact that she didn't have to worry about becoming pregnant--even if Ja-rael seemed to find that possibility distasteful.

He sulked. It irritated the hell out of Elise to find herself right back in the position of the 'invisible', but she felt like sulking herself so she pretended she didn't notice that he was studiously ignoring her again. Fortunately, it wasn't a situation she had to endure long. Three days later the green-blue globe she'd seen steadily growing closer filled the forward viewing port and she felt the pull of the planet's gravitational field.

Ja-rael sent her a speculative glance. "You should find a suitable place to secure yourself. We will be landing shortly."

Elise gaped at him with a mixture of outrage and horror. There was only one seat in the damned vessel and his ass was planted in it. Not that she had any desire to take his place! She couldn't land the thing!

Whirling, she made for the rear cabin. After glancing a little wildly around the nearly bare cabin, she finally grabbed the mattress and dragged it across to a table that was secured to the deck. Shoving the mattress under it, she used the linens to fashion a landing harness around her and the legs of the table, a job made more difficult by the fact that the ship had begun a tooth rattling shimmy and jolt before she'd even positioned the mattress. The jolting and bucking became worse. It reached a crescendo that had her fearing the entire ship would disintegrate around her and made her grateful for the padding the mattress offered.

A series of freefalls followed that almost made her lose the meal she'd had earlier. Her ears popped, adjusted to the pressure and popped again. Elise gritted her teeth to keep from biting her tongue, closing her eyes tightly as the battering became progressively worse. Terror clawed its way through her belly. She didn't know when she'd begun to mutter a litany of pleas like a mad woman, but when the vessel abruptly slammed into something and shuttered to a stop she bit a gash in her tongue. The taste of blood and the pain finally jolted her out of her terror sufficiently for her to realize that the vessel had stopped moving.

"We crashed!" she said on sudden realization, grappling frantically with the cloth she'd used to tie herself in and expecting an explosion momentarily. Finally, she managed to free herself and scrambled crab-like across the floor toward the door. Gaining her feet, she jerked the door open and charged down the narrow companionway. "Ja-rael! Run! It's going to blow!" she screamed as she reached the gangway.

Ja-rael, still seated in the cockpit, swiveled around to look at her in frowning curiosity. "We have landed."

Elise felt her jaw go slack. "Landed? *That* was a fucking landing? You call that a landing?"

He tilted his head. "We are on Meeri."

"We didn't crash?" Elise demanded in dawning fury.

Throwing off his harness, Ja-rael rose from the seat. "We landed," he repeated. "There is no danger."

"You *asshole*! *I* could have landed the thing as well as you did! Better! Why didn't you tell me you couldn't fly the damned thing?"

His eyes narrowed. "I am good. I have made many trips to Tor, and many back. The craft is still useable. If you like, I will show you."

Elise held out her hand as he strode toward her. "Not no, but hell no! I will never get on this damned thing again!"

He stopped before her, planting his hands on his hips. His lips tightened. "That will make taking you back to Tor difficult."

"I'll find somebody who *knows* how to fly," she said furiously.

"You will not."

"Yes, I will!"

He put his face down until it was even with hers. "Only pirates and thieves make the trip. You will find yourself bartered to the Torrines as a slave."

The comment effectively deprived Elise of air for several moments. She blinked at him several times while she assimilated that information. "You're a pirate?"

Chapter Fourteen

Ja-rael reddened. He straightened abruptly. "I am a trader."

"In contraband," Elise said tightly.

"...And a healer."

"Who pirates on the side. And you have the unmitigated gall to take the high ground on morality with me over sex?"

His eyes narrowed. "You do not understand--anything--my customs, my people--or me. You are in no position to make judgments."

"And you are?" she snapped.

He studied her for a few moments in tightlipped silence and finally sighed. "No. I am as guilty as you are."

It was probably as close to an apology as she was going to get, and not an especially grand gesture, but at least it said something for his reasoning. Elise struggled to tamp her fear and anger over the rough landing. "What now?"

He frowned, looking uncomfortable. "I must leave you here for a little while."

Elise's anger slipped upward a notch. "Why?"

"Because I can not take you into public like that," he said irritably, gesturing toward the robe she was wearing.

Elise lost her grip on her temper, mostly because it was very lowering to think he was ashamed to be seen in public with her. "Aside from the fact that I've got nothing else to wear, just what the hell is wrong with my appearance? What do you mean to do? Sneak me in under cover of darkness and hide me for a frigging year?"

He sighed. "I have tried to explain our customs. I know you don't fully grasp them yet, but you would not like the way you would be treated if you were seen dressed as you are."

"Fine!" Elise snarled. Whirling, she flounced toward the cabin. She wasn't certain what he meant by the comment, and she didn't feel any less insulted, but she was willing to admit, to herself at least, that the last thing she wanted was to attract unpleasant attention.

"I will return as quickly as I can. Do not leave the ship for any reason until I return," Ja-rael said as she slammed the door.

* * * *

Ja-rael felt the tension leave him as Elise closed the door. He'd feared that she would argue and that he wouldn't be able to make her understand that it was for her safety and protection, not his pride, that he wanted her to stay until he could provide proper attire for her.

Reluctantly, he realized his pride figured into it, too. That did not mean his motives were impure, however, only that he felt guilty that he even considered it as important as her comfort.

The thought irritated him, but he'd thought of very little else since they'd left Tor--when he could think beyond his hunger for her. She was his mate, like it or not. It was his duty not only to provide for her to the best of his ability, but to protect her to the best of his ability. She would not like to be shunned by his people only because of something so easy to remedy as her clothing and he would hate to see her treated in such a way.

He was torn, regardless of the reasoning behind his decision, because he also worried about leaving her alone and unprotected, even in the remote location he'd chosen to hide the craft. It would take a while to dispose of his contraband, even knowing where he could safely do so, and then he would have to go to market to find the things she needed. He'd calculated the risks, however, and decided it was the best choice of several unpalatable choices.

He didn't want to 'sneak' her in under cover of darkness for the same reason he didn't want to parade her in public improperly attired. It would appear that he had something to hide, or to feel shame about, which would result in the same situation. She would be looked upon as suspect, not welcomed as his chosen one.

Shaking off his uneasiness, he grabbed his herding stick and climbed down into the hold to round up the animals. The quicker he took care of his tasks, the faster he could return to his Leez.

If providence was with him, he could do everything and return before dusk the following day.

* * * *

Elise enjoyed her sulk until she heard the sounds that told her Ja-rael was leaving. Moving to the porthole, she stared out at the tangle of jungle just beyond the tiny clearing where the craft sat. Finally, Ja-rael came into view. He was using the strange lightning lasso-type thing she'd seen him use before to herd the animals.

She frowned. He'd said he was trading them for her. As insulted as she found that, she had to wonder why he'd changed his mind. It was *his* custom to pay a bride price. Had he decided there was no point in it since nobody claimed her? Since it wasn't the customs of her own people? Or because he'd decided she wasn't worth paying a bride price?

The last was a truly depressing thought. When he moved beyond her view, she sighed and flopped on the mattress, wondering what she would do with herself besides stare at the walls while she waited. She was tempted to go out to explore the new world, but not tempted enough to ignore the warning. Ja-rael had said not to leave the ship for any reason. She didn't think he would've said it if he hadn't thought it was dangerous to do so, and she had no idea what sort of wild life roamed the jungle that surrounded her.

She wasn't anxious enough to relieve her boredom that she wanted to risk becoming some predator's meal.

Finally, she decided to bathe. Ja-rael hadn't laid down any parameters about water usage, but she was keenly aware that she was an extra on the ship that hadn't been planned and she'd been afraid to use much when she had no idea how long it would have to last the two of them. They'd landed, so that was no longer an issue as far as she could see. The vaguely musky scent of their couplings still clung to her, or the cabin, or both. It wasn't an unpleasant odor by a long shot, bringing back memories that still sizzled with passion, but it affected her in a way she didn't currently find pleasing. She supposed it was only to be expected that they would find themselves on two sides of a fence at any time they weren't having sex. She could only begin to guess how different their cultures were--she suspected she only knew the tip of the iceberg--but it was already obvious they differed in their outlook on just about everything.

Sighing, she tossed the robe aside and went into the head to kill a little time in the bath. Her preoccupation made her careless. She stayed longer than she should have. The water dropped to a mere trickle before she'd managed to rinse away the soap. Dismayed, she sloughed off as much of the soapy water as she could and shut the tap, staring at it uneasily.

She was out of water and Ja-rael was gone. And she'd been so busy spiting him for making her mad before he left that she hadn't asked him when he thought he would be back.

Chapter Fifteen

Naturally enough, by the time Elise had dried and dressed, Ja-rael had long since disappeared. Elise stood at the porthole debating with herself for sometime, mentally imagining him moving further and further away and finally realized that her reluctance to go after him and admit what she'd done had condemned her to an uncomfortable wait.

He couldn't be gone long, she reasoned. He must have known the water supply was low and taken that into consideration before he'd decided to leave her.

Of course, he probably hadn't considered the possibility that she would go in like an idiot and squander what she had on a bath she could've waited on.

She hadn't been thinking very rationally. In all the time since they'd settled on Tor, water had been too precious to squander and everyone had known to be very careful with their ration.

It was really amazing and disconcerting to discover one could slip back so easily into bad habits.

Not that that realization was going to help her one iota and, naturally, the moment it struck her that she had nothing between thirst and herself but a few drops of water she began to feel very, very thirsty. She paced for a while, staring at the tap each time she passed through the tiny galley. Finally, she stopped and searched through the equally tiny cooling unit. Without surprise she saw that no beverage had magically appeared.

She was frightening herself for nothing, she chided herself.

Ja-rael wouldn't be gone long and if he was, well she wasn't helpless. She was in a lush jungle. There was bound to be water nearby.

She was completely unfamiliar with this world, however, and she'd gotten lost on the well worn paths in a familiar area, she thought glumly.

Thrusting that thought aside, she moved to the nearest porthole and studied the growth carefully, looking for some sign of open water. She'd made the rounds from one porthole to the next several times before a glint happened to catch her gaze. Relief flooded her as she stared at the rippling glint and realized it had to be sunlight playing on moving water. There was a stream fairly close by. It was hard to judge the distance, but it couldn't be far. Surely, if necessary, she could reach it and get back to the ship without any problem.

She wasn't especially anxious to try it, though. The light was already beginning to dim. She might not know much about nature, but she did know that animals tended to find the nearest watering hole at dusk and she couldn't think of any reason at all why that law of nature wouldn't apply to Meeri as it had on Earth, and Tor for that matter.

Relieved of that worry at last, her mind turned to her stomach. She'd grown so accustomed to hunger since they'd reached Tor that she tended to ignore it. Now that the danger of finding herself without water had passed, she left the porthole and went to search for something to eat. As careful as she was with her water supply, by the time she'd prepared the meal she only had a little over a half of a container of water to drink with it. Sighing, she mentally kicked herself again for her carelessness. She was going to be damned thirsty by tomorrow, and as reluctant as she was to risk a trip into the jungle, she had no choice at all.

* * * *

Elise woke with a raging thirst. It took an effort to gather enough moisture into her mouth to swallow. As reluctant as she was to give up the last remnants of sleep, she finally rolled out of the bed and headed toward the galley in search of something to quench the craving for liquid. There was very little left. Ja-rael had only brought enough supplies for himself for the trip, which had been divided by two on the way back and had quickly dwindled to the least palatable choices. She finally decided on something that looked and smelled like some sort of fruit--and not particularly pleasing--because the fruit-like things were all that were left. It was as tart as it smelled. She ate it anyway and felt marginally better when she'd finished it--thirsty but not quite as thirsty as before.

There were two more and nothing else.

She was going to be really pissed if Ja-rael didn't make it back soon, she thought irritably.

As tempting as the thought was to grab some containers and head for the little stream she'd spotted the day before, she decided to wait a while and see if Ja-rael came back before she was forced to the necessity of going into the jungle by herself. She spent most of the day pacing and watching for him. As the sun began it's downward trek, she was forced to accept that Ja-rael probably wasn't going to make it back to the craft before dark and she didn't think she couldn't handle another day without water.

Dismissing her qualms, she located the largest container she could find and moved to the mechanism that controlled the gang plank. When it had settled on the ground with a muted thump, she moved to the opening and glanced around uneasily. A cool breeze wafted across her skin. Elise shivered, her attention caught by the reviving coolness. She'd grown so accustomed to the miserable heat of Tor, she hadn't realized that it had grown uncomfortably warm inside the craft.

Glancing around with more interest now, she took a few, tentative steps down the gangplank and studied her surroundings cautiously again. The air filling her lungs was sweet, clean and blessedly cool. A sense of pleasure, carried by the pleasant breeze, wafted through her. "It's beautiful," she murmured in surprise. Was this unusual, she wondered, or typical? She couldn't recall ever feeling such a perfectly balanced temperature, not even manmade.

Feeling a sense of wonder, she moved down the gangplank and studied the world of Meeri for the first time with growing happiness. Who'd have thought such a world existed so close to the awful one their computers had guided them to?

Briefly, dudgeon filled her. "Typical! We could've had this! Instead, the frigging computer lands us on that miserable rock?"

She pushed the brief irritation aside. It was pointless. Undoubtedly, Meeri had been out of range when the computer had settled on Tor and just as certainly they had been beyond a lot of choices by that time. The ship hadn't landed gracefully. There'd been damage. It hadn't seemed to matter because they'd felt certain Tor was the best the universe had to offer them. Everyone was going to be severely put out when she got back and told them they'd landed on the hell side of Eden.

Or, maybe she wouldn't tell them. What would be the point? Making them *more* miserable? It wasn't like they had any way to change their situation.

Shrugging off her thoughts, she looked around again and saw that the sun was already lower than she liked. She shouldn't have waited so long, but she had no choice now. She was horribly dry. She couldn't wait until tomorrow to get water, or go back inside and hope Ja-rael made it back and could fetch water for her.

The jungle around her looked like a wall, though. She studied it for some time, trying to recall just where she'd seen the water. Finally, she remembered she'd seen it from the forward viewing port and moved around the vessel. There was no path, and no sign of the water from ground level. The stream hadn't looked like it was far away, though. Moving to the edge of the vegetation, Elise listened, peering through the gloom created by the thick tangle of growth. Finally, after studying the craft and the jungle, she decided she had the direction right and began to make her way cautiously through the undergrowth, glancing back every few moments to make certain she could still see the craft.

She'd been struggling against the tangle for perhaps fifteen minutes when she reached the point of no return. She could just barely catch a glimpse of the ship. If she moved deeper, she would lose sight of it and she could get lost. After considering it for several minutes, she looked around and decided to maintain the distance and move around the vessel. The stream had to be close.

She'd managed to break through about two yards of undergrowth when she tripped over a root and sprawled out, losing her grip on her container. The metallic clang sounded loud in the wooded area, seeming to echo almost as far as her squeak of surprise. "Well, if there were any animals around," she muttered as she picked herself up again, "that racket should have taken care of the problem."

It took her almost ten minutes to find the container again. By the time she had, though, she had heard the sound she'd been searching for--the musical tinkle of water trickling over the ground. Excitement went through her. Her throat almost closed with the thought of finally getting a decent drink of water. Throwing caution to the wind, she hugged her container to her and half fell and half stumbled through the undergrowth toward the sound. The water, she discovered when she fell in, was icy. She jumped up, gasping to catch her breath. Fortunately, the stream was shallow, stopping shy of her knees.

A chuckle of relief escaped her. Ignoring the leaves floating on top, she brushed them aside and drank until pain exploded behind her eyes from the deep chill of the water. Pinching the bridge of her nose, she fought a sudden wave of dizziness and looked around for the container she'd dropped when she'd sprawled headlong in the little stream.

Her heart stopped in her chest when she saw two golden, glowing eyes in the brush not ten feet from where she stood in the middle of the stream.

Chapter Sixteen

Elise's first, terrifying thought was that it was a predator.
It was, but not a four legged one. Her second, the moment
he stood up, was that it was Ja-rael, but that brief spark of
hope didn't last more than a split second. Her mind went
into shock, refusing to support her with any sort of
suggestions. Instinctively, she backed slowly out of the
stream. His lips curled in a feline grin that sent a jolt of
adrenaline pumping through her bloodstream. She let out a
scream like the wail of a siren and leapt from the stream
and up onto the bank. She was too panicked to think.
Blindly, mindlessly, she fled back the way she'd come.

She almost ran headlong into a second Meeri. She didn't
stop to think it over, but ducked, changed directions
abruptly and managed to elude him. Behind her she heard a
thud, the unmistakable pelting of flesh and realized the one
from the stream and the one she'd almost run into were
fighting--over her. She'd paused to catch her breath and
glance around frantically for the craft when she spied yet
another, or one of the first two, poised on the limb of a tree
at no little distance from where she stood. Panting now with
both terror and the need for oxygen, she changed directions
again and plunged onward.

She found the small clearing where the ship sat by virtue
of tripping over a root and plowing up the ground. When
she'd come to a dazed halt, she saw a patch of bare ground.
Scrambling to her feet, she raced mindlessly around the
vessel, hoping against hope that she wouldn't find yet
another one waiting for her and blocking her from the only
safety she knew of. There wasn't, but one rounded the end
of the craft racing straight toward her even as she pounded
up the ramp. She slammed into the bulkhead, unable to
slow her headlong dash enough to prevent the collision and
frantically tugged at the retracting lever. The gangplank
began to rise with agonizing slowness. It had only cleared
the ground by a few feet when one of the Meeri landed on
the end.

Elise stared at the man rounded eyed, trying to remember if there was anything even remotely resembling a weapon on the ship. Nothing came to mind, but as she glanced around for an alternative her gaze settled on the cooking vessel she'd used the day before. Grabbing it by the handle she raced down the rising plank. Two hands appeared about halfway down as another of the Meeri leapt up and grabbed it. With barely a pause, she swung the vessel, catching him on the side of the head with a loud clanging noise. He dropped like a stone. At almost the same instant, the one that had first threatened caught her around the waist. She butted him with her head, catching him on the nose. He released her abruptly, his hands going to his abused appendage. Before he could recover from his pain and surprise, she whirled around and swung her weapon again. It was a glancing blow, catching him on the shoulder before it impacted with his head, but the force was enough when coupled with the rising gangplank to knock him off balance. He fell, catching hold of the edge of the gang plank with one hand even as he toppled over the side. Elise dropped to her knees, whacking him a few more times for good measure and he finally fell free.

She slid into the ship off the rising gangplank and sprawled in the gangway, gasping for breath, but she saw with relief that the plank was almost vertical now, and mere inches separated her from safety. It closed at last, sealing her in and she breathed a sigh of relief.

Too weak and shaken even to consider trying to get up, she lay back against the cool metal, struggling to catch her breath. Her heart was still banging frantically against her chest, however, and it was some moments before she realized all of the pounding she was listening to wasn't internal. Finally, she struggled to her feet and hobbled to the nearest porthole. She couldn't see anything, but there was no doubt in her mind that the Meeri she'd met in the forest had followed her.

Shivering, she moved away from the porthole. They couldn't get in. Even if they knew the ship well enough to figure out where the external release was and how to bypass the code for the gangplank, she could block the manual operation and keep them out.

The only problem was, she was trapped inside and she had no water.

* * * *

Despite the skill Ja-rael had mastered with his herding stick, the animals were so terrorized by their ordeal in the hold of his ship that he had trouble controlling them. At first he was merely annoyed, but when dusk began to descend upon him and he still hadn't reached the buyer an uneasiness began to creep over him that he had trouble shaking. He wasn't accustomed to indecision, particularly when he knew he'd thought a situation through carefully and considered every conceivable possibility, but he found himself worrying about Leez in spite of every effort to dismiss it as unfounded.

His abstraction cost him. A beast broke free and he lost more time rounding it up again. Dark caught him still in the woods and miles from his buyer. When visibility became so poor the animals kept running into the trees, he allowed them to rest and settled beneath a tree to sleep until the twin moons of Meeri rose. As short as the rest was, it refreshed him and he made far better time when he set off once more, arriving at his buyer before the moons had set.

The sun had risen by the time he'd completed his business and set off again. As weary as he was from little rest, though, he made far better time without the beasts to contend with and reached the city late in the afternoon. Anxiety had caught up with him again, largely he suspected, because of his weariness, but he had expected to reach the city early in the day, find what he needed to for Leez and return to her sometime in the evening. Already he had been away a full day and a half. Even if he rushed to complete his business and made good time going back, two full days would have passed.

With an effort, he dismissed his qualms, concentrating on the task of finding clothing he thought would please Leez that were fine enough to be worthy of his mate.

He discovered it was not as easy a task as he'd thought it would be. He did not care for the color of this. The workmanship of that was poor. The quality of the fabric of this robe was far too rough for her delicate skin. Finally, he settled not very happily on the best that he could find, had his purchases bundled and glanced at the market clock. His heart failed him. The sun was already dipping toward the horizon and he very much feared that, with the best will in the world, it would be morning before he returned to the ship.

Ja-rael was in such a rush to leave the market, he slammed into a man heading in the opposite direction. Begging pardon, he took a step back and tried to go around. It was several moments before he realized the man was deliberately blocking his path.

"Ja-rael! Thank Minoa I found you! I've been looking everywhere for you!"

Ja-rael stared at the man for several moments before a spark of recognition dawned. He plastered a perfunctory smile on his lips, searching his mind a little frantically for the man's name and coming up empty. "I've been away-- bartering for a mate."

The man stared at him blankly for several moments, glanced at the package under Ja-rael's arm and finally emitted a stilted laugh. "And you succeeded, yes? I can see you're anxious to get back to her."

Ja-rael's responding smile was a little easier that time. "Yes," he admitted, trying not to sound as anxious as he was. "She is the most beautiful creature under Minoa's sun."

Clautz--Ja-rael finally recalled his name--forced a grin. "I have no doubt, and you of all those I know deserve to find such a prize."

Every man claimed his mate was beautiful beyond compare, and very likely many thought so, for any mate at all was a gift from Minoa, but it rarely transpired that everyone agreed with the fortunate male once they'd seen his prize. Ja-rael could see the skepticism in this man's face and a sense of pride filled him, and amusement to imagine what Clautz would think when he saw his Leez, who truly was so beautiful she could take one's breath. "You must bring your mate to visit her once we have settled."

Clautz's face fell. "She is not well. That is why I've been looking for you so desperately. I know you have your own business to attend to at the moment, but please--just come and look at her and tell me she will be alright and I won't trouble you further."

Concern instantly supplanted his anxiety to be gone. "What is wrong?"

Clautz glanced around and lowered his voice. "She labors to bring our off-spring into this world, but it seems to me she has labored far too long. I expect I am over-anxious, it being our first ...."

Ja-rael felt his heart clench, but he couldn't recall that Zelia was due to deliver any time soon. "How long?"

"Since yesterday."

Ja-rael relaxed fractionally. "It is a long time to labor, but it is her first also. Very likely there is no problem, but I will come with you and have a look at her."

The man's sense of relief was such that Ja-rael could see he was controlling the emotional wave that followed it only with an effort. "Yes! Thank you! I've brought my glider and won't detain you long."

Ja-rael shook off both the thanks and the apology and followed Clautz quickly to where he'd parked his glider. When he'd stowed his package and climbed into the passenger seat, Clautz opened the solar sails and within moments the sleek craft had lifted away from the market and shot toward the northern perimeter of the city. Twenty minutes later the craft settled on the square before Clautz's domicile with a heavy thud. Ja-rael exited quickly, more because of his relief that Clautz, who'd exhibited his anxiety in hair-raising flight, had managed a safe landing than his worry about the patient. That changed the moment he was ushered into Zelia's chambers. He scarcely recognized the writhing, bloated creature on the great bed in the center of the room. Striding toward her, he leaned over the bed and began to speak to her soothingly while he examined her. "Zelia, what happened?"

She opened her eyes to look at him. He saw recognition, and then her gaze slid away. "I don't know," she said plaintively.

Ja-rael caught her jaw, forcing her to look at him. "You do know. You were not due to deliver for weeks. Has--did Clautz do something?"

Zelia opened her eyes long enough to focus on Clautz accusingly. "Besides this, you mean?" she said, gesturing toward her bloated abdomen.

Ja-rael straightened, his eyes narrowing on Clautz. "Did she fall?"

Clautz looked terrified. "Ja-rael! You know me! You know I wouldn't harm her. I love her with every fiber of my being! How could you even think I'd do anything to harm her--especially now when she is so fragile?"

Ja-rael studied him hard for several moments, but he could see nothing to indicate Clautz was being evasive or dishonest.

"He wouldn't let me go to the King's celebration," Zelia gasped.

The comment brought Ja-rael's head swiveling back toward her sharply. He leaned toward her again, speaking low now. "What did you do?" he asked harshly.

She wouldn't meet his eyes.

He caught her jaw again, forcing her to meet his gaze. "You know I will find out--but it could be too late to help you. Tell me!"

"I took melanine--just a small amount to make me a little ill so that he would be sorry he'd been so mean."

Ja-rael felt a little ill himself. "How small an amount? When?" He knew it was pointless to ask, however. It had induced her labor early and Clautz had already said that she'd been laboring for a full day. It was far too late to try to get it out of her system. He could do nothing now but try to repair whatever damage she'd done to herself.

He was relieved, however, to discover it actually had been a very small amount. If she'd been so foolish and spiteful as to have taken more there would have been no hope for her or their offspring. As it was, he had grave doubts the cub would survive.

When he glanced at Clautz again, he saw the man was looking so crushed he seemed in imminent danger of needing medical attention himself. "Clautz!"

Clautz's head jerked up and he stared at Ja-rael in blind terror. "Is she--," he paused, licking dried lips, "will she be alright?"

Ja-rael fought a round with his temper. "It was a stupid play for attention--but I think it will be alright. Go to my home and bring my instruments." When Clautz merely stared at him blankly, he repeated the command, adding, "it will be much better if I stay with her than you."

Nodding jerkily, Clautz yanked the door open and fled.

A sense of despair swept over Ja-rael as the man left. His Leez was alone. What if she needed him?

He shook the thought off. As far as he knew, she was probably suffering from nothing more than boredom. He couldn't leave a woman he knew to be in need of his skills as a healer only because he was allowing his imagination to wreak havoc with his nerves.

Chapter Seventeen

The scent of males drifted faintly past Ja-rael's nostrils. He paused jerkily, breathing more deeply. The scent was stronger then, giving the lie to the possibility that it was merely imagination, and rife with lust, both bloodlust and desire. As remote as the area was, Leez had been discovered.

Feeling a surge of adrenaline rush through his bloodstream despite his nearly unbearable weariness from four days of nearly no sleep and the exhaustion of expending so much effort in healing Zelia and her cub, Ja-rael dropped his packages and began to race along the almost invisible trail he'd been following through the deep woods. He skidded to a halt when he reached the clearing where he'd left his craft.

A large male was perched on the top of the ship, his heels braced against the lip of the gangplank as he tried to force it open far enough to climb inside.

"She is *mine*!" Ja-rael roared furiously.

The male had been so intent on what he was doing, he hadn't even glanced up at Ja-rael's arrival. The roar of challenge caught his attention instantly, however. Snarling, he leapt from the vessel and landed in a half crouch in the dirt beside it. "She is unclaimed!"

They launched themselves at each other then, colliding almost mid-air with a meaty thud before they hit the ground in a furious tangle and began wrestling for dominance. Weapons of any kind were forbidden and the male had already slashed Ja-rael along his side before he realized the male was armed. Surprise and then a fresh burst of fury washed through him. The blood he'd smelled made more sense now.

Grabbing the wrist that held the blade, Ja-rael surged upward, forcing his opponent over. Following as the male lost his balance and landed on his back, Ja-rael scrambled on top of him, straddling his opponent's waist and pinning him to the ground with his weight. When he'd gained dominance, he tightened his fist around the wrist he held, trying to paralyze the male's hand. Growling like a beast, the man clung to the blade with desperation, trying to wrench free.

Gritting his teeth, Ja-rael squeezed harder, resisting every effort the other man made to buck him off. Finally, the blade dropped to the ground. Ja-rael scooped it up in a flash and dug the point of the blade in the male's chest just deep enough to show him he meant business. "Yield! Now!" he growled through gritted teeth. "Or I swear by Minoa I'll cut your heart out. I am a healer. I can remove it from your chest so quickly you will live to see me crush it!"

The fight went out of the male abruptly. "She was alone!" he said in a panting breath.

"But claimed, and you damned well knew it!" Ja-rael said furiously. "You simply chose to ignore my scent!"

The male looked away guiltily. After a few moments, Ja-rael eased the pressure against him. When he made no attempt to renew the fight, Ja-rael withdrew. The male studied him for several moments and finally scrambled to his feet and ran, disappearing into the thick woods.

Panting, Ja-rael got to his feet with an effort, watching for many moments to make certain the challenger wouldn't return. When the male's scent dwindled, he glanced down at the wound on his side and examined it. The gash was bleeding profusely. A wave of weakness washed over him. Closing his eyes, he concentrated with an effort. It was muscle tissue. No vital organs had been damaged. *Cease!* He commanded. His heart ceased to pound within his chest. The rhythm slowed to normal, and then dropped lower still. Pulling the two sides of the wound tightly together, he held his hand over it, commanding the flesh to mend. Ten minutes passed, fifteen, and then he began to feel the painful tightness as the new flesh entwined with the injured flesh. Cautiously, he pulled his hand away. The wound burned as the flesh tugged, trying to separate, but it held.

Ignoring the pain, he looked around at the clearing and then up at the gangplank. It had been pried open nearly six inches, he saw. If he'd been any longer in returning, the male would have had her.

Fresh anger went through him. With an effort, he tamped it and moved to the exterior control, keying in the security.

The panel opened, but he discovered to his dismay that the mechanism was jammed and refused to respond to the controls. "Leez! It is I, Ja-rael."

He listened, realizing for the first time that a deathly quiet had fallen over the clearing. "Leez!" he called, trying to keep the fear out of his voice.

He held his breath, listened acutely, but could not hear so much as a tiny rustle of movement. Fighting panic now, he moved back from the vessel, gauged the distance to the top of the gangway and launched himself toward it, catching the edge with his fingers. His side burned. As he scrambled to climb the slick side of the vessel, he felt a tear as the tender flesh gave way again and the warmth of new blood flow. Gritting his teeth, ignoring the burn, he struggled until he'd managed to lever himself onto the lip. When he'd braced himself and pushed at the gangplank for a few moments, he felt it give slightly. Stopping, he examined the opening and decided it was wide enough he could squeeze through. The blood slickened him enough to allow him to force his way through, otherwise he wasn't certain he would've made it.

As he dropped to the gangway, his gaze flickered over the mechanism. He saw that one of the cooking vessels had been wedged between the gears, preventing the hatch from being opened completely. A faint smile curled his lips. Clever!

"Leez!" he called again, glancing around. When there was still no answer, he headed for the cabin.

She was lying on the bed, and so still his heart seemed to stop in his chest for several painful moments. He wasn't even aware of surging toward her, only of falling to his knees beside the bed and lifting one limp hand. Her skin was hot and dry. For a split second, relief filled him when he realized she was alive, but she was perfectly limp and unresponsive. Placing her hand on the mattress once more, he lifted her eyelids, ran his hands over her. Her lips were dry and cracked.

A sickening thought occurred to him abruptly. Leaping to his feet, he strode quickly from one tap to another. Nothing but the sucking sound of air greeted him, not even so much as a single drop of water.

Cursing, he ran back down the gangway and wrenched the pot from the mechanism, pulling the lever to lower the gangplank. To his relief, it responded, sluggishly, bumping and halting, but it began to sink toward the ground. Grabbing a vessel from the galley, he ran down the plank, leaping to the ground and racing toward the stream nearby. The first thing that caught his eye when he reached the stream was the gleam of another vessel lodged against debris along the bank. He stared at it for several moments, then glanced around, fighting the anger that was quickly overshadowing reason. The brush was trampled in every direction. The mingling scents of four distinct males lingered lightly in the air.

She'd tried to get water and they'd been waiting for her!

For several moments, he couldn't think at all. Such rage filled him that it threatened to completely consume him. The urge was strong to set out after them at once and tear them limb from limb. He stared blindly at the vessel digging into his palm from his tight grip. Leez was in serious trouble now, dehydrated, quite possibly beyond his ability to heal her. If he allowed his rage to control him, he would be condemning her to certain death.

Battling his rage to a standstill, he bent and scooped water into the vessel and hurried back to the ship.

* * * *

"Thought you weren't coming back," Elise muttered when she felt the blessed coolness of a cloth on her skin.

Ja-rael almost dropped the cloth from suddenly nerveless fingers. "Leez?" he murmured, hopeful, but disbelieving.

She didn't respond and he simply stared at her for several moments, wondering if she'd actually spoken or if his exhaustion had made him hallucinate it. He had not slept for more than a handful of minutes in so long that he had no idea of what day it was or how long he'd been struggling to coax Leez back from the brink. He'd used everything he'd ever been taught to treat her and watched fearfully to see if she would respond. She did, but sluggishly, not nearly as well as he'd hoped, convinced himself that she would. The fear seized him and grew upon him that she was not even his kind. He knew nothing about treating humans. What if he was doing everything wrong? What if it was not enough? Too much? Or just the wrong thing entirely? He was just as fearful of trying to draw upon his inner healing. What if her physiology was so different he harmed her instead of helping?

Desperation had goaded him into trying. When he'd delved her mind in search of her spirit to aid him, he had felt the oneness that had mated them, had been certain that he was helping, but that had been at least a day ago and she had not appeared much improved.

He sat back on his heels wearily, silently commanding her to say something, to let him know that he hadn't simply imagined that she'd spoken.

He saw the movement of her throat as she swallowed. "Thirsty," she said, her voice plaintive, as hoarse and cracked as her dry lips, but unmistakable.

His heart squeezed painfully in his chest at the single word. A knot formed in his throat. Swallowing against it, he laughed a little shakily and bounded to his feet, snatching up the drinking vessel he'd left hopefully nearby. Scooping an arm around her shoulders, he lifted her carefully and placed the rim of the vessel against her lips. She took a sip that was almost microscopic, swallowing with a painful expression. Frowning, he insisted that she drink more. She complained but yielded to his demand until he was finally satisfied.

When he'd set the glass down once more, he climbed onto the bed beside her, sprawled out and lost consciousness. Movement shook him awake sometime later. His eyes felt as if they'd been glued shut, however. His body ached it every place that contained a nerve ending and his head felt as if it would explode. It took a tremendous effort to pry his eyelids open a slit to stare blearily, and without immediate comprehension at the ceiling above him. The bed shook again, drawing his attention, and he turned his head to see Leez struggling to sit up.

He shot up from the mattress as if he'd been catapulted upright, memory instantly flooding back. "What are you doing?" he demanded harshly.

Elise subsided, but obviously from weakness rather than from any concern about his displeasure. "I need to go," she said irritably.

Shrugging off the aftereffects of such a deep sleep and swift awakening with an effort, Ja-rael slid to the edge of the bed and placed his feet on the floor, holding his pounding skull. "Go where?" he growled, equally ill-tempered.

When she didn't answer, he dropped his hands and lifted his head to look at her questioningly.

She reddened. "Go--you know?"

He stared at her blankly for several moments before comprehension dawned. "You shouldn't be up yet. I'll get you something to use," he added, standing with an effort and wavering almost drunkenly on his feet.

"Don't you dare!" Elise snapped.

He stared down at her in dawning anger. "You're in no condition to get up!"

"I know whether I can get up or not."

His eyes narrowed. "So do it," he suggested tightly.

Glaring at him, her anger and determination helped her to struggle upright and throw her legs over the edge of the bed. Gasping as if she'd run a mile, she pushed herself up on shaking legs. Ja-rael grasped her shoulders, steadying her.

"Are you going to help me?"

"No."

Elise glared at him and sat back down weakly. "If you bring me a bed pan, I'm going to clobber you with it," she threatened.

They stared at each other angrily for several moments. "Alright," Ja-rael conceded finally. "I'll help you, but if you feel like you're going to faint, sit down on the floor and call me. Is that clear?"

Relieved, Elise nodded. She was so pale by the time he'd helped into the facilities, he was loath to leave her. Determination was evident in her expression and every line of her body, however, and finally, very reluctantly, he departed and left her in peace. When he heard her at the door again, he opened it, scooped her into his arms and settled her on the bed again. After she'd drank a full tumbler of water, he left her to rest and retreated from the room to wrestle with the demons that had been torturing him in his dreams.

One thing had become crystal clear to him. He had been criminal in taking Leez from her people--and he had no right to take a mate, at all, let alone Leez, whom he had put in grave danger simply by removing her from all she knew and abandoning her in an unknown place. His duty was to protect her, but as a healer he had an inescapable duty to his patients, as well. When the conflict between his dual obligations had arisen, he had failed his mate and she had nearly died because of it.

He stared blindly at the darkening landscape beyond the viewing port, wondering which was going to be worse, living with Leez for a whole year, knowing he must take her back--or living without her afterwards.

Chapter Eighteen

As much as Elise enjoyed being waited on hand and foot, and fussed over, by the end of the following day she was beginning to chafe at Ja-rael's determination to keep her in bed. She still felt like hell, but she knew from experience that the only way to regain her strength was to get up and move around. She finally decided she was just going to have to 'sneak' or Ja-rael was going to make her stay in bed for the rest of her life.

The first few trips she made from the bed to the facilities and back, she staggered so much that Ja-rael heard her and came to investigate--and treated her to a tirade on her 'childishness'. It infuriated her, but his concern was strangely warming, too, particularly since he was behaving so oddly.

She finally decided he must have figured out what she'd done and he was angry that she'd behaved so stupidly it had almost cost her her life. If true, she supposed it was only to be expected that he'd treat her like a willful, thoughtless child.

He seemed so uncomfortable around her, though, that she began to wonder after a couple of days if it was guilt that was riding him, if he felt like it was his fault that she'd nearly died of dehydration.

"It was my own fault, you know," she said tentatively when he brought her food on the third day after she'd awakened.

He glanced at her sharply. "Why would you think that?"

She shook her head and grimaced. "I squandered the water on a shower. I know it was stupid not to check first. I wasn't thinking."

He studied her for several moments. "It would not have been an issue if I had not stayed away so long."

Elise frowned. "How long?"

He rubbed his head. "I don't know. Days, much longer than I intended. I--I did not sleep much, which made it difficult to track the time."

Elise digested that in silence. "Something happened."

He shrugged, but his lips tightened in repressed anger. "A patient--spoiled, stupidly willful female. She had taken something to spite her mate for not letting her have her way and nearly died and killed her cub, as well. The cub may not survive anyway. It was forced into the world early by her carelessness." He paused for several moments. "If you are well enough to travel tomorrow, I need to get back to check on the infant."

Elise nodded, but she was too appalled by the story to make any sort of comment. No wonder he hadn't slept! A niggling of guilt flickered through her. She wondered if she'd sounded accusing when she'd asked him why he'd been gone so long. "Oh," she managed to say finally. "Uh-- I think I can manage. Is it far?"

She could tell by the way he was looking at her that he was wrestling with some internal debate. "Not far," he said finally. "I can carry you to my glider."

"Glider?" she asked.

"The vehicles which we use to travel in on Meeri," he responded shortly, turning to leave.

He paused in the doorway, looking uncomfortable. "I appreciate it more than I can say that you are too good hearted to blame me for failing you, but I can not so easily dismiss my responsibility." He sighed gustily, paused hesitantly for several moments and finally spoke again harshly. "I have come to realize that there is no place in my life for a mate. I release you from the promise I forced you to make. I will not expect you to accept me as your mate and I will return you to your people as soon as I can. In the meanwhile, I hope that you will allow me to accept the responsibility of your welfare until I can take you back."

Elise was still gaping at the door when he closed it behind him, too stunned to think of anything at all to say. She sat pondering his comments for some time, trying to figure out why she felt like crying and what, exactly, he'd meant. No place for a mate? Did he mean he'd decided she was totally unsuitable? Or was he still feeling guilty about her getting herself into such a fix?

Most importantly, why did she feel like she'd just been rejected? And why did it bother her so much? She'd intended to go back all along. She'd figured he would see

the futility of the situation long before the twin worlds
came into proximity again.

She hadn't expected him to see it the minute she did
something that was, admittedly, one of the stupidest things
she'd ever done. She still couldn't figure out why she
hadn't even thought to *check* the water supply before she'd
taken the notion a bath would make her feel better, but that
was beside the point. Perfectly intelligent and responsible
people died from stupidity all the time, just because they
were distracted and not being as careful as they should be.

He had a hell of a nerve making that kind of snap
judgment about her anyway! She was no fool. She was
educated *and* intelligent *and* she came from a civilization
worlds more advanced than his!

How *dare* he imply that she wasn't good enough for him!

She knew that was it. He'd gone into the city, looked
around at the other cat people and thought about the fact
that she was going to be a freak among them and he was
too embarrassed by his lapse in judgment to admit he was
ashamed to show her, ashamed to claim her.

The asshole!

* * * *

Elise had her first suspicion that she might have judged a
little hastily herself when she finally got a look at the glider
Ja-rael had spoken of. This was no primitive mode of
transportation. She'd more than half suspected the glider
was even some sort of domesticated beast of burden and it
was startling enough to discover it was actually a machine.
It was far more than that, however. It was a beautiful piece
of technology. The reddish metal it had been constructed of
gleamed brightly in the light of Meeri's sun. It was as sleek
as a bullet and Elise had an uneasy feeling that it would
move like one, too.

She discovered with more than a little dismay that she was
right. When they'd strapped themselves in, Ja-rael began to
press buttons and levers. A gleaming, metallic solar sail
appeared, pulling energy from the sun. Moments later, the
small craft rose from the ground. When they reached a level
just above the tops of the trees, the craft blasted forward as
if it was a stone slung from a sling shot. Nausea threatened
to gain control of Elise for several dizzying moments after
take off. Finally, she mastered it, soothed the tight knot in

her stomach, and peered around her nervously. In the distance, she saw tall, spires and strange, bulbous roofs capped with needle sharp peaks. As they neared the city, she saw a number of other crafts similar to the one she was in zipping back and forth across the airspace above the rooftops.

"My god!" she breathed with a mixture of awe and disbelief. "It's ... it's beautiful!"

Ja-rael flicked a glance at her. "You thought we lived in huts?"

Elise reddened. She could see from the derisive amusement in Ja-rael's eyes that she'd given her thoughts away and felt hotter color fill her cheeks. "No," she lied. "I just never expected anything like this."

He didn't believe the lie. She didn't have to look at him to know that much, but her discomfort was leavened with the anger that had kept her silent during the time since he'd spoken to her the day before about taking her home. Whatever she'd thought, she reasoned, he'd done nothing to make her think otherwise. He was attired now in a long, flowing robe and loose legged trousers, but he'd been wearing a loincloth when she'd met him. In hindsight, she supposed that was due to the heat on Tor, and possibly because the Torrines actually *were* a more primitive race, but he'd had every opportunity to disabuse her mind of her misconceptions when he'd been teaching her his language and customs. He hadn't made any effort to describe the society he hailed from beyond that.

They'd crossed the city and neared the outer edge before the craft began to drop toward the ground. It settled with a tooth jarring thump on a neatly trimmed square of greenery, beside a half dozen similar crafts, although most were easily twice the size of the craft Ja-rael flew. As unfamiliar as she was with the vehicle, Elise had the impression that there was more of a difference than the size and suspected, as nice and well maintained as it was, that Ja-rael's was the economy version.

The landing clenched an earlier impression she'd had of Ja-rael. He seemed competent enough once airborne, but he was obviously a seat-of-his-pants pilot and landing was definitely not his forte.

Belatedly, she recalled that she'd sworn he would never get her off the ground again in anything he was flying, but she'd been too pissed off and too surprised at the sight of the vehicle to recall the vow.

The landing jarred it into her memory.

Elise was still struggling to climb out on unsteady legs when she noticed that doors and windows had opened in many of the neat domiciles that surrounded the square. Within a few moments, a half a dozen younglings of varying ages tumbled out of the buildings and scampered in their direction like a pack of jubilant puppies. Behind them, parents followed more sedately.

To Elise's stunned surprise the younglings, laughing and chattering happily, launched themselves at Ja-rael as if he was some long lost relative. He laughed, catching them against him in affectionate hugs, rubbing a hand over one's head, patting another on the back. Elise was so transfixed by the laugh that she was scarcely aware of the fact that the adults had halted some distance away to stare at her as if they'd never seen anything like her.

Which they obviously hadn't.

Ja-rael, glancing up from the children, studied Elise for a moment, then looked at his neighbors. His smile faded. Disentangling himself from the youngsters, he moved to stand beside Elise, placing a hand along her waist. "Leez, these are my neighbors," he said, his expression conveying a brief warning that she found impossible to interpret as he turned and introduced them by name. Most of them simply continued to gape at her. A few managed polite smiles that looked more stunned than welcoming.

"She is maned," one of the males said blankly, then turned a deep shade of embarrassment when both Elise and Ja-rael glanced at him. "You said she was beautiful, Ja-rael. You did not tell me she was a maned lioness. Great Minoa! Where did find ... I beg your pardon! Please accept my apologies for being so rude."

Elise glanced at Ja-rael uncertainly. His hand tightened on her waist. Ever so slightly, he shook his head. "Many sectors from here, beyond the dead lands."

The women began to chatter far too fast for Elise, with her limited knowledge of their language, to keep up.

"No wonder you were away so long!" the male Ja-rael had called Clautz said in amazement. "I had no idea you traveled so far to trap."

Ja-rael shrugged. "Much further this last time than ever before."

"And the hunt went very well, for you got your bride price, I see."

Ja-rael looked uncomfortable, but it was obvious even to Elise that bragging about the value of their mates was expected. "Thirty zihnars."

There were gasps of amazement all around. "Truly?" one of the youngsters asked. "You found thirty and you traded them for her?"

Ja-rael smiled at the small female, patting her head. "Truly." He squatted down before her. "And I was terrified that it would not be nearly enough."

The child giggled and flicked a glance up at Elise. "Because she has the mane?"

Ja-rael's smile faded. Giving the young female a pat of affection, he straightened. "Because from the moment I saw her I knew that she was the other half of my soul and that I could not live without her."

Chapter Nineteen

Elise could've said with absolute certainty that her arrival and introduction ranked as the most awkward moments in her life. She was pretty certain it would've been uncomfortable anyway, but there were more recent factors that made it worse because she was now as acutely conscious of Ja-rael's discomfort as her own.

She knew why he'd lied about where he'd found her. Self preservation was a strong motivation when the alternative was criminal charges and she was fairly certain a society as strict as this one seemed to be would not turn a blind eye to trafficking in illegal goods. She supposed it was for the same reason that he hadn't admitted that she was no maned lioness. Obviously doing so would have aroused suspicions. Her being here might do so anyway. She was too different from everyone else *not* to be noticed where ever she went, and speculation was bound to follow.

Why had he allowed them to believe she was his mate, though, when he'd told her that was no longer something he was interested in?

Wouldn't it have just been easier all the way around to make up some other kind of story to cover her presence? Wasn't it going to be even more awkward for him when she disappeared again?

Or maybe not. Maybe he figured he could just tell them a partial truth--that she'd returned to her own people?

But why flowery speech about love?

Her Meeri might not be all that great yet, but she'd followed well enough.

She glanced up at him speculatively as they left the group and crossed the green toward one of the smaller domiciles on the square. Tension radiated from every line of his body despite the fact that his expression was carefully neutral.

Maybe it was just the way these people spoke? The one called Clautz had been very elaborate in the way he spoke, particularly when he apologized. Not simply a 'sorry' and a shrug, but a scrupulously worded apology.

She was almost disappointed when she came to that conclusion, but it seemed inescapable given what she'd learned about their speech patterns, and she hadn't really believed it any of the time, she told herself. Love at first sight was a wonderful fantasy belief a lot of people indulged in, and it had certainly been proven that, scientifically speaking, two people sometimes connected instantly on a chemical level. But that wasn't really love. You couldn't love someone you didn't know.

Besides, she and Ja-rael weren't even the same species as far as she knew. Even that sort of chemical 'love' couldn't be possible, could it?

Who was she kidding? One blast of his pheromones and she'd been putty in his hands and permanently, she feared, addicted. Obviously, the same could not be said for him, though, or he wouldn't have calmly informed her that he'd concluded that it just wasn't going to work out for him.

Or maybe he'd had a similar chemical reaction, but he'd had enough time to get to know her to decide she just wasn't his type?

Lowering thought.

Maybe she shouldn't have been such a pushover? Apparently the women on his world had 'hard to get' down to a science. So, like anything else that was too easy to get, he'd been thrilled until it had dawned on him that it was too easy and therefore couldn't possibly be the prize he'd thought it was.

That was an even more distressing thought.

She was almost relieved when Ja-rael helped her mount the shallow stairs leading to the house.

The door was not locked. He simply opened it and ushered her in. Surprised, Elise couldn't prevent the question that popped into her mind. "You don't lock your doors?"

He looked equally surprised by the question. "Why would I lock the door? It is my home."

Elise blinked at that, several times, but decided she wasn't going to admit that thievery was so common among her own kind that it was the only way to be sure you'd still have something when you returned home.

A big city, full of people, and he didn't lock his door. More than that, he was surprised enough she knew it wasn't the exception, but the rule.

She shrugged, dismissing it. "Why didn't you tell them I'm not a lioness at all?"

His flesh darkened. "I told you. Trade with the Torrines is forbidden. I've no desire to rot in prison only because...."

He stopped abruptly, leaving the sentence hanging.

"I grasped that part. But you could just as easily have told them that you'd found *my* colony in the lands beyond the dead lands--where ever that is, which I assume is some where on this planet."

He threw her an uncomfortable glance.

"You didn't want them to know I was ...." Elise stopped as a peculiar notion popped into her head. "An alien," she finished. "I'm the alien here. Strange, but I never felt like an alien on Tor." She thought that over for several moments. "I guess that was because I was still with my own people."

His lips tightened. "Yes. I expect that is it. And Minoa willing, none will learn before you leave so you will not be treated as an outsider."

There were undertones to his comment that disturbed her and made her certain that she wasn't entirely right about his reasons even if she'd guessed a part of it. Instead of pursuing the matter and risking making things more uncomfortable between them, she decided to change the subject. "Who or what is this Minoa everybody keeps talking about?"

"The mother of Meeri and of us all."

Elise gaped at him. "You're not serious? Like a god or I guess goddess?"

He frowned at the unfamiliar words, but Elise realized she'd learned nothing in either language to help her to translate. "The spirit you pray to? Worship?"

He smiled faintly. "Once. Now it is only something we say." He glanced around the narrow hallway where they stood as if seeing it through a stranger's eyes. "This is not grand, but I hope that you will find it comfortable."

Elise followed suit. If by grand he meant large, then that was certainly accurate. On the other hand, the hallway alone was as much space as she'd had for her private use so it looked pretty roomy to her and from where she stood she could see several comfortable sized rooms opening off of it. If he meant rich, then that was true also, but neither was it mean or dirty or ugly or utilitarian as the habitat was, no matter how much effort they put into trying to make it feel and look like 'home'. "It's lovely."

He nodded.

She placed a hand on his arm. "I mean that. It is a lovely place. Was it like this when you came to live here? Or did you do all of this yourself?"

He seemed to relax. "I like these colors."

"I do, too," she said sincerely, glancing around again at the vivid blues and greens that covered the walls that she could see.

He seemed pleased. "I had thought---never mind."

Elise frowned. "What?"

"I have only myself to please," he said finally, his voice flat and unwelcoming. "If you are tired, I will show you your room."

She was tired, she realized. She'd just been too tense since they'd left the ship in the woods to realize it. "Yes, please."

Nodding, he guided her toward the rear of the hallway and opened the last door. Elise moved to the doorway and peered in. The walls were colored in the same vivid blues and greens as the hallway. Heavy fabric, in a corresponding shade, covered the two tall windows that were centered in both exterior walls. Between the widows was a large bed, the frame of which seemed to be wrought of metal. Tall, twisting pillars formed the legs which supported the large mattress off of the floor and spiraled upward to support a canopy. Fabrics like that which covered the windows was draped across the upper supports and down to the floor, tied by matching strips of cloth to each of the four corner posts.

Tiles or some kind of stone covered the floor, but here and there were small rectangles of lush fabric carpets. A small table, wrought of the same metal, stood near one side of the bed and held a medley of personal objects. As she stepped inside the room, Elise saw that a tall chest, or perhaps something like a locker, took up much of the interior wall nearest her. Along the adjacent wall was a desk and chair and at the foot of the bed a low chest. She moved toward the nearest chest, the one that stood at the foot of the bed and ran her hand over it curiously. It was cool to the touch, but not like metal. "What is this made of?"

"Lintron," Ja-rael responded almost absently, moving toward the tall cabinet and opening the doors. "The wood of a tree."

Elise was almost as horrified as she was fascinated. "A living thing?"

He threw a frowning glance in her direction. "A renewable resource. We husband them carefully. If we are not wasteful, then all that we have will be here for many generations of Meeri to enjoy."

She saw that he was removing clothing from the cabinet. "This is your room," she said with sudden conviction.

"For now, it is yours."

"But--I'd really feel a lot better if you'd just put me somewhere else."

"You are my--guest. This is the best I have to offer. It is yours."

Chapter Twenty

It was more than just a relief to discover she'd been so very wrong about the civilization Ja-rael was taking her to. It was stunning. The city was a real, honest to god modern city. The women did not wear veils, at all. In fact, although their clothing was very similar to that worn by their male counterparts in design--they all wore long, flowing robes, or tunics, over loose fitting trousers--the fabrics they were made from were often so sheer the females who wore them were the next thing to naked.

They did not travel under guard, and although she learned very quickly that it 'was not done' for a female to travel alone, she could see the sense of that.

Her wonder, and surprised pleasure, at her changed circumstances pretty much began and ended there, however.

In the space of fourteen days, Elise had learned that the Meeri calendar contained fourteen months. Each month was divided into 24 days and each day into 30 hours. She learned this not because it was something of tremendous importance to her but because she was so bored she had nothing better to do with her time. Within the first six days--which constituted a Meeri week--she had recovered completely from her illness and begun to pace Ja-rael's domicile until she knew every inch of it as well as she knew her own private cubical in the habitat. She had learned the verbal and written language of the Meeri well enough to read the labels on everything in the house and talk to herself in that language.

Ja-rael was rarely at home except when he slept, breezing in occasionally during the day to grab something or check his communications to see if he had any emergencies to attend to and then leaving again--and sometimes leaving at dawn and returning way into the night for days on end. At first she thought little of it. She was merely disappointed that there was no chance to pursue the important issue of whether or not she was willing to concede to his wishes regarding the mating business. She knew he'd been gone a very long time and she'd learned from her interaction with the neighbors that the city boasted only a small handful of healers. There were bound to be a lot of things even beyond attending his patients that he needed to take care of. She sought patience and waited.

When a month had passed, she finally accepted that Ja-rael had no intention of allowing her to compromise the decision he'd made. Unfortunately, she had also come to the conclusion that she wanted the chance he'd offered to make it work out between them. Part of it was the fact that it hadn't taken her five seconds to realize being with him meant more physical comfort than she'd known since she'd left Earth, but as appealing as that was she was pretty sure she would've wanted to stay anyway, even if his world had had no more to offer than the habitat, or even as much.

She didn't know exactly how she felt about Ja-rael beyond an almost painful physical attraction, mostly because he refused to satisfy her cravings--apparently since he'd decided they weren't going to be mates, he saw no sense in mating at all--but she'd come to realize that she had enjoyed all of the time she'd spent with him, even when they'd been arguing-- enjoyed it enough that she missed being with him so much that it was almost a physical ache, enjoyed it enough to know that a lifetime of it was something to fight for, not against.

How was she to do that, though, when he seemed determined to treat her like a complete stranger and to distance himself from her until the bridge they'd begun to build between them collapsed from neglect?

He was not human, but as far as she'd been able to tell from the little interaction with his kind that she experienced, the Meeri were subject to the same emotions and motivations as humans--which seemed to her to indicate that what she knew about the human male should also apply to the Meeri male. The females of the neighborhood were pampered, spoiled and lazy as hell. Beyond attending their young and their household, they did very little else –and they were as bored as she was, maybe more bored because the customs of Meeri left them little outlet to express themselves. Consequently, they generally behaved abominably, going out of their way to annoy their mates just to get a little attention.

Elise was contemptuous of them at first. After a full month of cleaning things that didn't need to be cleaned, staring at the walls, and reading the labels on containers, she was beginning to see their side of things.

Ja-rael had given her the only bedroom his home boasted and decamped to the couch in the living area. She avoided him as assiduously as he avoided her at first, embarrassed to be such an inconvenience, angry with him for withdrawing, but when nearly a month went by and she saw nothing would change unless she made it change, she decided to lay in wait for him.

She didn't want to be too obvious--not obvious enough that he'd see right through her machinations. On the other hand, the experience she'd had with human males had led her to the conclusion that subtly simply went right over their heads.

In the end, the opportunity she'd been looking for simply landed in her lap.

Although she generally gave up on Ja-rael and went to bed before he even came in most nights, she'd decided to stay up and wait for him and take it from there. When she heard footsteps on the walk, and then the porch, her mind simply went blank and she began casting around frantically for something she could say that wouldn't make it obvious that she'd simply been waiting for him.

To her surprise, instead of the door opening, someone rapped at the panel. Startled, she jumped to her feet and rushed to the door before she'd even considered that it might be dangerous to simply open the door so late in the evening when she was all alone. One of the neighbors, Clautz, whose wife had recently given birth, stood on the stoop. He looked disconcerted to discover it was she who'd opened the door. For several moments he merely blinked at her with his jaw at half mast.

"I beg your pardon for disturbing you at such an hour. Might I have a word with Ja-rael?"

Elise could feel color flooding her cheeks. "He isn't home yet."

Clautz seemed disconcerted by the news. He frowned and glanced around uneasily.

"Would you like to come in and wait for him?"

His eyes widened until they looked in imminent danger of popping from the sockets. "NO! Excuse me. Pardon my outburst, please." Several emotions chased across his face. "Forgive my impertinence, but this is not acceptable."

"What?" Elise asked blankly.

His flesh darkened. "Ja-rael has explained that your customs differ--but it is not acceptable for a male not a family member to visit in the house of another male if he is not present."

"Oh." Elise reddened. It wasn't really acceptable in her culture either if it came to that and could lead to all sorts of nasty rumors and suspicions. "I only thought--well, you must have something important...?"

"If I could trouble you to pass along a message to him?" he asked finally.

"Certainly."

"He was to have come tomorrow to examine my male child, Sadiem, but I have been called away on business and we will not return until Muncing. If he would please come the following day, on Vincing, it would be greatly appreciated."

Elise smiled as it sank in that he'd handed her the perfect reason to be waiting for Ja-rael. "Certainly! Thank you!"

He looked puzzled.

"For letting us know."

He still looked confused. "Of course, it is only polite to do so."

And the man was excruciatingly polite. Instantly, it popped into her mind to wonder if he was as polite in the bedroom. She could imagine how thrilling it must be for his mate--Pardon me, but could you please move your leg a little to the right? Would you object a great deal if I placed my phallus in yours?

She bit her lip to keep from chuckling at the thought and bid him a good evening. When she'd closed the door, she released a snort of laughter and quickly covered her mouth, hoping he hadn't overheard her. Returning to the living area, she entertained herself for the next little while envisioning all sorts of exquisitely polite scenarios. She was still snickering over it when Ja-rael came through the door.

Instantly sober, she wondered if he'd overheard her sitting on the couch alone and giggling to herself. He'd think she had gone mad.

One look at his face was enough to tell her he had and that what he'd imagined hadn't been at all pleasant. He glanced around the room suspiciously, as if he more than half expected to find a randy male hiding somewhere in the room. Elise didn't know whether to be more pleased by the sign of jealousy or annoyed by the lack of faith. "Looking for something?"

He frowned. "You're alone?"

"He climbed out the back window," she said provokingly.

His eyes narrowed.

"Of course I'm alone. I'm always alone." She bit her lip. She hadn't intended to provoke a fight. What was the matter with her?

"Someone was here."

It wasn't a question. It was a statement of fact. Elise looked at him in surprise, realizing that he was tense all over--a sign of both anger and battle readiness. "How would you know that?"

"The scent lingers. I know this scent."

Elsie felt her jaw sag. "You *smell* his scent?" she asked, torn between disbelief and horror at the very thought that he had such an acute sense of smell. That certainly answered the fidelity issue on *this* world!

He really was angry. It was the first time she'd ever seen him angry and she found it more than a little unnerving.

"He didn't even come in," she added hastily. "The neighbor, Clautz, came to speak to you."

"And lingered when he was told I was not here?"

"You're starting to scare me," Elise said uneasily. How the hell could he tell that? "He just wanted to let you know he had to go out of town for a few days," she added, deciding that this conversation was going nothing like she'd planned. "And now that I've told you I believe I'll go to bed."

She thought for several unnerving moments that he wasn't going to let her pass. Finally, with an obvious effort, he forced himself to relax and moved aside. He caught her arm as she brushed past him, however. "Leez."

She looked a question at him.

"I beg your pardon."

She stared at him a long moment. "Well, you don't have it, damn it! You've got no reason at all to have such nasty suspicions about me ... except that *you* ignore me all the time!"

He darkened with color, but held his temper. "I am a healer. My duty is to see to the needs of my patients."

Elise's lips tightened. "Lying obviously isn't confined to humans. These people are so damned healthy it's almost nauseating! I haven't seen one sick person since we've been here. How can you possibly be busy from daylight till all hours of the night?"

He sighed tiredly. "You see only the well-to-do. The poor live much further from here and they have many and varied illnesses, and injuries can happen to anyone anywhere."

"You're saying you're gone all the time because you go to all these places where there are sick? Aren't there any ... uh ..." She frowned. Hospital was one word she hadn't learned. "Buildings where all the sick and injured are taken?"

He looked taken aback. "You can't seriously think those in need of a healer should come to me so that it is more convenient to me?"

Elise blinked in surprise, floored by the notion. She had never even heard of medicine being practiced any other way than what she'd known all of her life--and that was to move all the sick and injured to a specific location for treatment. She'd never questioned the practice, but even if she had she knew it was easier to keep all of the medicines, equipment, nurses and physicians in one place and have everyone come to it, or be brought to it. She supposed, though, that there was a lot to be said for Ja-rael's practice, as well--or, she supposed, the way the Meeri practiced healing. Moving people who were seriously ill or injured was rarely the best case scenario.

She shook her head. "No. You're right. You're a healer. You life isn't your own and it sure as hell can't belong to anyone else."

A sense of hopeless filled her as she stalked down the hallway and into the bedroom, slamming the door behind her. First he suspects her of screwing around behind his back and now she was just a nasty selfish bitch!

Well, that settled that, didn't it? Short of contracting some hideous disease or dismembering herself, it didn't look like Ja-rael was going to have time for her in his life.

She supposed that was why he'd said there was no place in his life for a mate.

Bullshit! He'd found the time to hunt and trap, hadn't he? He'd managed to find the time for illegal trade with the Torrines. She knew he was a healer and a lot of folk depended upon him for their very lives, but as busy as he no doubt was, he was taking advantage of the situation. She knew was.

She just didn't know what she could do to change his mind about her, but somehow she doubted fighting with him was going to get her what she wanted.

Chapter Twenty One

It wasn't until Elise woke the following morning that it occurred to her that she hadn't given Ja-rael the entire message. She spent most of the day digging up the yard to work off her frustrations and excess energy and waxing hot and cold on whether or not to wait up for Ja-rael again to give him the rest of the message. In the end, she didn't make a decision at all. She'd spent so much time destroying the neat little yard that surrounded Ja-rael's domicile that she was out like a light as soon as she'd had a shower and eaten.

* * * *

Misery, Ja-rael reflected wearily, was a relative thing. Why was it, he wondered, that one always thought one had struck bottom only because of some fairly insignificant setback or roadblock? The truth was, no matter how low one seemed to get, there was always more room at the bottom.

He had only thought that he was miserable having no one of his own. As much as he had tried not to envy those with a mate and family, his position prevented him from avoiding constant contact with those who had what he wanted so badly until he'd become obsessed with the determination to change his situation.

And now he had.

And he had never been more miserable in his life, but he was afraid even to accept that assessment for fear it would get worse.

It would. He knew it would when he took Leez back and the only thing he could think of to do to minimize the pain was to make certain he didn't grow too accustomed to having her around to start with.

It had seemed a sound idea at the time, but he could not say that the effort was going that well. Thoughts of Leez dogged him throughout the day, and even though he rarely caught more than a glimpse of her, or exchanged more than a few words with her in a handful of days, he was excruciatingly aware of her presence in his house. Her enticing scent seemed to linger in the air to tease him from the moment he entered the house until he left it. Everywhere he looked, he saw the signs that said they lived together--and yet didn't--things that had been moved, water droplets in the shower from her bath, the smell of food she'd cooked.

He stepped in the hole before he even realized there was a trap waiting for him in his own front yard. The drop was only a few inches, but in his abstraction it was enough to throw him off balance and it was only by luck that he managed to keep from sprawling headlong in the yard.

When he'd caught his balance, he looked down at his feet. Sure enough, the walking stone was gone. Glancing around now, Ja-rael saw that the entire yard had been desecrated. He muttered a string of oaths beneath his breath, feeling his weariness and depression instantly transformed into anger.

She'd destroyed his carefully maintained yard!

She'd done it for spite. He knew that right away.

Spoiling for a fight, he stalked up the steps and slammed into the house. He was both surprised and more than a little disconcerted when he discovered that Leez was not waiting for him, a satisfied smile teasing the corners of her lips. Thwarted of an immediate target for his temper, he paused in the doorway, listening acutely to the sounds of the house. Her scent lingered in the air as always, but there was no sound to indicate her presence.

Closing the door with less violence than he'd used to open it, he moved from room to room and finally paused at the bedroom door. It was closed. It was always closed, a constant reminder that he was not welcome even if he so far forgot himself and his position as to cross the line he'd drawn for himself.

Grinding his teeth, he pushed the door open.

She was sprawled on the bed, apparently dead to the world. He studied her suspiciously for several moments, certain she was only pretending to be asleep. He could see nothing to substantiate the suspicion, however. There was no sign of tension at all. Her breathing was slow and even.

Contrarily, that pissed him off more. She'd not only destroyed his yard, she'd come in and gone to bed as if she was completely innocent of anything at all!

Uttering a low growl of frustration, he stalked to the side of the bed.

"What have you done to the yard?"

Jerked awake by the sound of his voice, Elise cracked one bleary eye at him. "I'm redoing it," she muttered.

That calm announcement deprived Ja-rael of words for several moments, but it also gave him time to consider if he hadn't been a little hasty in his immediate conclusion. She was obviously worn out from the effort of destroying the yard, but he couldn't see anything in what she'd said or her attitude to indicate that she'd deliberately caused mayhem to annoy him. The reflection didn't make him any less angry, but it made him more cautious. "I almost broke my neck in the hole you left where the walking stones used to be."

"Sorry," she muttered without much contrition and rolled over. "Fix it tomorrow."

Ja-rael stood over her, staring down at her angrily, but feeling a surge of satisfaction, as well. She *did* want a fight! She'd willfully destroyed the yard and now expected him to take time off from his patients to repair the damage? He didn't think so! She'd done it. *She* could repair it! "I have to see a patient in the morning," he said finally.

"I'd never have guessed it. *I'll* fix it."

He was almost disappointed at the response. It completely took the wind out of his sails and left him no where to go with the fight he'd been spoiling for. He looked her over, assessing, considering whether to pursue the argument anyway. It was a lapse in judgment. He saw that when she rolled over the loose robe she was sleeping in, exposing one shoulder and a breast right down to the pink nipples that fascinated him. His throat went dry. His mind went blank.

Abruptly, he whirled on his heel and retreated.

* * * *

The following morning Elise dragged herself out of bed and staggered into the facilities. The thing she loved most about the little house that was Ja-rael's was that the bathing facilities were the most wonderful she'd ever in her life experienced. Even before they'd left Earth, water had been a problem. Purifying the water supply was so expensive, and so absolutely essential, that bathing with it had been outlawed most of her life. Even the oldest of homes had been outfitted with particle showers and for those who remembered bathing in water, it was a piss poor substitute.

Ja-rael's house--she supposed all homes on Meeri--was equipped with a purifying system far superior to anything she'd ever known and recycled the cleaned water through the house over and over without wasting more than a few drops. She could take a shower as long as she wanted--which she frequently did.

When she'd finished, she went into her second favorite room--the cooking area--which was also technologically superior to anything she'd ever seen. There she made herself a cup of what she liked to pretend was coffee--she'd been pretending she had coffee so long that she couldn't even remember what it actually tasted like--and then went outside to sit on the stoop and sip it while she surveyed her handiwork.

Several of her neighbors were standing at the edge of the yard gaping at it when she arrived. She waved at them gaily and sat down anyway.

Embarrassed at being caught gawking, they moved on with their offspring.

She couldn't say that she blamed them. The yard looked like hell--like there'd been a major battle. Briefly, she felt guilty about it, but she dismissed it. When she was done it would look fine. And then she would start on the backyard.

She'd just taken a sip of her hot drink when a memory that had been floating hazily around in her brain finally solidified. She choked, coughing for several moments before she managed to bring up the liquid that had gone down the wrong way.

Ja-rael had woken her the night before about the yard.

A faint smile curled her lips and she sat pondering the situation for a while. She hadn't really considered when she'd been doing it that Ja-rael might object, or that it would be something to get his attention. She'd just needed to do something.

Maybe, instead of wasting so much time trying to think of some subtle way to waylay Ja-rael when he came in at night, all she really needed to do was make it impossible for him to forget her presence?

She suffered a qualm or two over the idea. He'd told her she was a guest, and what she had in mind--what she'd done already--was not the sort of thing a guest should consider if they wanted to remain welcome.

He'd said before, though, that she was his mate. He'd insisted on it, in fact, in spite of her protests. He couldn't undo that, could he?

And, if she was his mate, then she had as much right to decorate as he did, didn't she?

She studied the butchered yard for several moments and finally decided she did.

Setting her cup aside, she went into the yard to decide how she wanted to arrange the stepping stones that led from the road to the house. Every single residence around the green had virtually identical yards. Everything was absolutely symmetrical. The walk divided the yard in half and went straight up to the stoop. Nothing but the grasses they used for their lawns broke the monotony and the grass was a monotony in and of itself.

She decided a curving walk would be much more pleasing. It might not be quite as efficient since it would take a few more steps to reach the stoop, but what difference did that make when it would be prettier?

First though, she decided she needed plants, flowering plants. She knocked on three doors before one opened to her. She smiled at her neighbor, cast around in her mind for a name and came up blank.

"Hello! I'm Elise, Ja-rael's ... mate. We met when I arrived?"

The female smiled back. "Yes. I am Kloe. May I help you?"

"Actually, I was hoping you could. I want plants for our yard."

Kloe blinked several times. "Plants?"

"Yes. To make it pretty."

Kloe frowned. "The grasses have died?"

Elise chuckled. "Not yet. I just dug it up. I want flowering plants."

"Oh."

She sounded more confused that enlightened, but Elise supposed that was because none of the houses on the green had them. "My people use them to decorate."

The female nodded as if that explained everything, but she still looked confused. "We don't."

Elise smiled with an effort. "But I do. I don't suppose you have any idea where I could get some--plants, I mean?"

"The forest?" Kloe said doubtfully.

"Not at the market?" Elise countered, feeling disappointment overshadowing her enthusiasm.

"We go on Cincing. You can go with us tomorrow and look," Kloe offered.

It seemed doubtful she would find what she wanted there, but Elise thanked her and, after asking what time they would be going the following day, returned and set to work on the walk way. She was exhausted by the time she'd managed to shift the heavy stones to form the pattern she wanted, far too tired to consider doing anything else and it was growing too dark to work outside anyway.

As tired as she was, she still felt better than she had in a very long time, more content and light hearted. Brushing as much of the dirt and grass off as she could, she headed inside and soaked until her skin had pruned and she'd removed every speck of soil from beneath her nails. When she'd finished her solitary meal, she went into the living area and looked around until she found the writer, which was actually very similar to those designed by Earth technology, and sat down to play with it until she decided she had the hang of it. She was still trying to decide which layout she liked best when she heard the door open and then close.

Glancing up, she saw that Ja-rael was standing in the doorway. Smiling at him absently, she returned her attention to the writer.

"You said that you would repair the damage to the yard."

"I did," she said without looking up.

"There are holes."

"Oh. Sorry. I didn't get around to filling them in. Tomorrow--wait, maybe not. I'm going to the market tomorrow with Kloe and some of the others."

She could feel his gaze on her and after several moments she set the writer aside and got up, stretching to relieve her cramped muscles. A wave of warmth flowed over her, followed by that chemical scent that made everything inside of her clench. With an effort, she pretended she hadn't noticed. "Sorry. Guess you're ready for bed. I'll just take this in my room."

Grabbing the tablet up, she strolled past him without a glance and down the hallway. The faint dizziness had passed by the time she closed the door behind her, but the craving hadn't. It destroyed any hope of concentrating on anything else. Finally, she set the tablet aside, commanded the lights off and climbed into bed. Sleep was slow to come, though, because she imagined she could still feel Ja-rael's desire.

The following morning, Elise took her tablet and her 'coffee' out to the stoop and sat down to study her plans and her progress on the yard. She was pleased that the walk looked far better even than she'd realized the evening before--maybe the stones weren't entirely level but it shouldn't take much to remedy that--and she wondered if she could find some sort of small plants to border the edges--perhaps taller grasses?

The females were chattering almost excitedly when she joined them mid-morning. She assumed it was because of the trip to market--sad thing when a trip to buy food was the highlight of the week--but since the chattering stopped abruptly at her approach she revised that assumption.

They'd been talking about her.

Smiling with an effort, she greeted Kloe. Kloe re-introduced her to the others--Sinata, mate to Timus, who lived across the green from Ja-rael and owned a house twice as large, and Ania, mate to Mazel, who owned a larger house still. The females seemed friendly enough--in a snotty superior sort of way.

"Zelia usually goes with us, but her mate, Clautz, has taken her away for a few days," Kloe added as they turned and began to follow the road toward the heart of the city.

"I know. Clautz told me. Ja-rael was supposed to check on their ... uh ... newborn."

The females exchanged a look. "Clautz told you?"

Elise gave her a look, firmly tamping the irritation that surfaced. "He left the message for Ja-rael. Whose glider are we taking?" she added, changing the subject abruptly.

The reaction to that question only irritated her further. Kloe merely gaped at her. Ania and Sinata snickered. "Do the maned lioness' use their mate's gliders?"

Elise opened her mouth to demand to know why the gliders would be exclusively for the use of the males and then shut it again as it occurred to her that she was going to have to live around these females a long time--even if Ja-rael took her home, longer if she had her way. "You mean you don't?" she countered.

"Oh! I couldn't possibly...."

"I'd be terrified even to try it!"

"This is so very strange! Do the females do all of the work?"

"Why would you ask that?" Elise demanded, irritated in spite of every effort to remain civil.

Sinata gestured toward the yard as they passed it. "You were seen."

Else frowned. "And?"

The females exchanged glances. Sinata sniffed. "We are far too delicate for such labor. Males have the strength to do such things."

Elise gave Sinata a once over and refrained from pointing out that a little exercise wouldn't do her any harm.

"Ja-rael claimed your bride price was thirty zihnars. Is it true?"

Elise fixed the female called Ania with a hard look. "Are you suggesting he lied?"

Ania turned red, made several aborted attempts at speak and subsided into silence.

"You mustn't mind Ania," Kloe said soothingly. "She doesn't mean to be rude. She just can't seem to help herself."

Ania sent Kloe a look that was part embarrassment, part resentment. "I beg pardon. I didn't mean to insult you. It's only--well it is so huge a bride price. And no one I know commanded such a price--And Ja-rael is a healer, after all."

"Meaning?"

Kloe shrugged, drawing Elise's attention from the stammering Ania. "Healers forgo wealth in the pursuit of their calling, for they must heal any in need and, unfortunately, the poor are more in need. He is a very good male, and we are blessed to have him--so you must not think we mean to insult him. Undoubtedly, he is also a very skilled trapper to have managed to capture so many of such a rare beast."

Or desperate.

Elise hadn't really given much consideration to that particular custom, aside from being insulted about Ja-rael's assumption that he could buy her. She glanced back at the little house nestled between two far larger homes. It was, in fact, the smallest of all the homes on the green.

But it wasn't like he'd needed a lot of room. He had no family. Until she'd arrived, he'd lived there alone.

And it was a very nice little house.

She could tell they felt very superior about having larger houses, though.

Ja-rael didn't seem to mind that he had fewer and less elegant possessions than his neighbors. He seemed devoted to his practice, devoted to his patients.

Except that he'd wanted a mate so desperately that he'd been willing to risk being jailed for trafficking with Torrines in order to raise the money for a bride price.

The thought dulled her enjoyment of the unaccustomed treat of an outing.

Chapter Twenty Two

Elise had just stopped before yet another stall in the market place when she felt an unmistakable tug on her hair. It didn't hurt. In fact, it was almost unnoticeable, but she had felt a similar touch at least a dozen times in the hour they'd been wandering around the market. Even though it didn't hurt, that time she turned to glare at whoever had sneaked a surreptitious feel. Ania snatched her hand back guilty.

"I beg your pardon. It's just---is it hot?"

Elise frowned in confusion. "Because it's red, you mean?"

Ania looked equally confused. "Not the color. It covers your head and neck and then grows down your back and it does not appear to be light like the clothing we wear. I thought it must keep you warm."

Elise couldn't help but be indignant. "It does not grow down my neck and back!" She lifted the hair to show Ania that it was only attached at her scalp.

Ania stared at the fall of hair in awe. "It grows so long!"

Elise smiled wryly. "And fast. If I don't cut it soon it'll be down to my ass."

"You mean it just keeps growing?" Ania asked disbelievingly.

"Of course...." Elise broke off. Ania wouldn't know. None of them would. She was the only 'maned lioness' any of them had ever seen. "Yes. But it isn't as heavy as it looks and it doesn't make me hot--at least most of the time it doesn't." She lifted a lock of hair and allowed Ania to examine it.

Eagerly, Ania grasped the strands of hair, rubbing it between her fingers and then stroking it. "It's so soft!" she said in a breathless voice. "It's beautiful. I do wish--but envy is an ugly thing. My pardon. You must be very proud of it?"

Elise chuckled and finally shrugged. "To tell you the truth I never liked the color much. I always wished it was sleek and black and silky--like my mother's."

The young female gaped at her. "There are many colors? But--would that not look strange? It would not match the hide, surely?"

Elise burst out laughing. "The ... uh ... hide comes in many colors, too."

Ania's look was disbelieving, but she chuckled, as well. "Now you are teasing me."

Elise shook her head. "I'm not. I swear."

Ania still looked doubtful, but she smiled. "I'm sorry about--the things I said a while ago. Kloe's right. I don't mind my tongue as I should, but I truly didn't mean to insult you."

"It was just as rude of Kloe to point it out," Elise said, her amusement dissipating.

Ania covered her mouth to hide a smile. "You are as bad as I am! Shhh! She will hear you."

Elise shrugged unconcernedly. "She and Sinata are too busy talking about everyone else to hear anyone talking about them."

Ania bit her lip to keep from smiling. "I like you, Lise. I can see why Ja-rael adores you so. You are not only beautiful, you are clever and funny and you have a very good heart, just as he does. I am so glad he found someone like you. He was so lonely and I would have hated it for him if he had had to settle for someone like--like Kloe or Sinata. Not that they are so terrible, mind you! It's just-- well they are very spoiled and self-centered. I do not think they would even mind their young except that it is expected for a female to be devoted to her offspring."

"And they are very careful to behave as expected?"

Ania nodded. "Their mates are high in the government of the city. My Mazel is only a clerk so I am at the very bottom of the social scale."

Elise's brows rose. "Where do healers and their mates fit into the scale?"

Ania looked at her curiously. "They have no true standing, but they are honored and respected by all so they have no need of it--nor wealth either. To be truthful, Ja-rael is respected more because he is not wealthy. Not all healers honor their vows as they should. Many times I have heard Kloe's mate, Jida, say to him that he must insist upon receiving fair pay for his services, even from the poor, that they are only pretending they have nothing to pay with so that they can keep their tavos to spend on hard drink. Ja-rael is always polite, but I can see it makes him angry."

"What do you think?"

"I think that I know nothing of the matter--and neither does Jida, for his family has been wealthy for generations. He can not make a fair judgment on a life he has never led. And I also think that you are the luckiest of females, for Ja-rael is not only handsome, but clever and ..." She stopped self-consciously. "Did that sound very bad? I suppose it did, but it is not what you think. He has been my healer since I was a child and though I do not feel anything forbidden, I do admire and respect him more than anyone I know--except my mate, of course."

Elise smiled with an effort, but it was hard to tamp the unpleasant knot of jealousy in her stomach. She would've had to have been a complete moron not to know that Ania worshiped Ja-rael, but perhaps it was more admiration that affection for him as a male, just as she claimed.

All the same, females had been known to confuse the emotion with true love more than once and when it came right down to it the hair's worth of difference rarely mattered.

"I haven't seen the first plant," Elise said, changing the subject abruptly.

Ania blinked, but followed Elise's lead readily. "No. I beg pardon. I knew you would not when Kloe told us that was why you wanted to come, but I wanted the chance to get to know you so I didn't say anything. Besides, there are many beautiful things here for you to buy."

Elise shrugged. Ja-rael had bought her more than enough to wear. She never went anywhere so there seemed little point in spending the tavos he'd given her on more, particularly since she now realized how hard he worked for them.

"The things he bought you are beautiful. I had no idea he had such wonderful taste! But you will want to buy things more to your own taste." She chuckled. "I was here the day he came. It was so amusing to watch him studying each thing so carefully. And everyone was very curious because we did not know he had a mate to buy for. Not that Mazel would do such a thing for me. He has far more important--uh--what I meant to say is that ...."

Elise couldn't help but be amused at the dilemma Ania's swift tongue had gotten her into. Either *she* wasn't important enough to her husband for him to spend so much time on her, or Ja-rael's time wasn't important enough. Insult herself? Or insult both Elise and Ja-rael. "Never mind. I get the idea. Where do you think I might find plants?"

Ania frowned, looking around the huge market at the many stalls as if she expected the plants to magically appear because there was a demand for them. "The forest?"

Elise shook her head. "I can't believe no one here cultivates plants purely for their beauty."

Ania chewed her lower lip indecisively for several moments. "The thing is, we do not believe in exploiting nature. We prefer to live in harmony with it to the best of our ability--only tampering where absolutely necessary."

Elise had been half heartedly examining the wares of the stall they had stopped in front of--a maker of shiny, metallic vessels for all sorts of uses--but at that she glanced at Ania sharply. "They *are* living things, but they grow as happily in one place as another."

Ania's face darkened with embarrassment. "I hope you'll pardon me for being so rude. I didn't mean for it to sound like that. It's just--long ago, in the days before the tribes of Meeri warred and divided, we took what we wanted and wasted what we did not and our world suffered for it. It was a very harsh lesson, and one we do not allow ourselves to forget. So now we are very careful with everything because we realize we do not really understand the delicate balance and can not hope to control it."

Elise's interest was piqued. "You seem like such a--polite, peaceful people. I can't imagine the Meeri warring."

Ania shrugged. "Now we are. When you are careful of the feelings of others then it is possible to for many to live closely together and still maintain harmony. The time I spoke of was so long ago--to be honest, I had always thought it was merely tales that had been passed down to teach us the lessons we needed to learn. I suppose everyone did until Ja-rael brought you here. According to the legends, the maned lions were one of the three tribes of

Meeri, and then there were the people who called themselves the Torrines. Our world divided in war."

Elise blinked several times. "The world broke apart?" she said, aghast, wondering how it was even possible that they'd literally blown the world apart and any of them had survived.

Ania giggled. "I didn't mean the planet. I meant the people. The three tribes were all so different, they couldn't agree upon anything and they broke apart, each settling far away from the others. Were you not taught this, also?"

Elise definitely did not want to get into that kind of discussion. Ania's tongue was loose on both ends. It didn't take a rocket scientist to figure out that anything that went into her head would come spilling out sometime. "Is it forbidden to transplant?"

Ania looked confused for several moments, but then frowned thoughtfully when she recalled the discussion they'd been having about the plants. "I'm not sure."

"A law?"

Ania's brow cleared. "Neither Kloe nor Sinata said so, did they? It must not be forbidden."

"But then they knew I wouldn't find plants here," Elise pointed out.

Ania shrugged. "Yes, but they would still have said something. They consider themselves the 'guardians' of proper behavior---you noticed they *did* comment on you working in the yard. Ladies are not supposed to labor. They are only suitable for light work."

Elise let that pass. She'd do what she damned well felt like doing. If she chose to do it, she didn't figure it fell under the heading of anyone else's business. From what Ania had said, Ja-rael had no real social standing anyway. It wasn't like anything she did would hurt him socially and it was obvious they expected her to be strange.

As conceited as it sounded, she was probably the most entertainment they'd had in months--or cycles as the Meeri referred to them.

Now all she had to do was figure out how she was going to get to the forest to collect the plants she wanted when it was forbidden for a female to travel alone.

* * * *

Elise had been struggling with leveling the walking stones for hours and had gotten so frustrated she'd given up a half a dozen times. Each time she plopped down on the stoop to glare at the things, however, she realized she was just too stubborn to allow the task to defeat her and after resting a few moments she would get to her feet and try again.

The sounds of an arrival late in the afternoon dragged her attention from the stone she was worrying with and she glanced around to see Clautz returning with his family. She was about to return her attention to her task when she caught motion out of the corner of her eye and looked instinctively to see what it was.

Ja-rael!

Two thoughts collided in her mind almost instantaneously. Ja-rael had returned early--and he was heading right straight for Clautz. In about five seconds he was going to find out she hadn't delivered the message that she'd been given.

She'd forgotten it the first time because of the argument she'd had with Ja-rael. The second opportunity had been missed because she'd been too groggy with sleep to think of it. There hadn't seemed much point in telling him after that, but she realized now that there had been a point-- reliability. It hadn't seemed all that important, but it wasn't her place to decide on the importance of a message meant for someone else.

She flushed guiltily when the men, who'd met in the front yard, glanced in her direction. Pretending she hadn't noticed, she did her best to concentrate on what she was doing. A few minutes later she heard the faint, but unmistakable, tread that told her of Ja-rael's approach.

* * * *

"Greetings! I hope that your trip went well?"

Clautz smiled at Ja-rael. "Indeed--and I take it from that that your lovely mate, Leez, did convey my apologies? I did not like leaving when you were expected, but I had no choice. And you were not home.... Will you be coming by tomorrow, then, to see little Sadiem?"

"Yes. I am anxious to do so. He has seemed to be thriving well?"

Clautz looked uncomfortable. "Yes. Zelia is--we are both embarrassed about her behavior, and also most grateful that you were there for us in our time of need. As angry as I was with her when I discovered the foolish thing that she had done, it made me see that there is little point in succeeding well in my job if I fail my family."

Ja-rael nodded, but he wasn't certain he completely agreed. It did not seem to him that Clautz was in any way to blame. He pampered Zelia outrageously.

Clautz frowned, looking even more uncomfortable. "And how are things going for you and your mate?"

Ja-rael felt his belly clench uncomfortably. "Well," he answered.

Clautz nodded, seemed to debate with himself and finally spoke again. "I hope that you consider me a friend?" he asked hesitantly.

Ja-rael looked at Clautz in surprise, feeling the knot in his stomach tighten even more. Such prefixes generally preceded comments that were personal and rarely welcome. "I do," he responded uneasily.

Clautz reddened. "I have wondered if I should say anything at all, but I do value you highly, Ja-rael, and I would not wish to see you unhappy."

Instead of commenting, Ja-rael lifted one brow questioningly. His expression, however, was far from welcoming.

Expelling an uncomfortable breath, Clautz persevered anyway. "The ladies talk. I have overheard some comment that you seem--not completely satisfied with your mate. I say this as a friend, because I know that you have been very busy since you returned and perhaps have not realized that they will take their lead from you. She will not be accepted by the others if they believe you regret having taken her as your mate."

Ja-rael reddened with both anger and embarrassment. It wasn't as if he had not known that that would be the case, but he had not realized that he and Leez would be watched so closely that the neighbors would see that he went to great pains to avoid Leez. He should have known better! The females had little to do with their time beyond gossip!

But it had been no part of his plan to make Leez the butt of gossip or the recipient of their cold shoulders. It did not matter that she would be leaving. He did not want her to be unhappy while she was here, and he could not think she would be happy if her overtures of friendship were shunned out of hand only because he was so weak where she was concerned that it was easier for him to avoid her than to control himself.

As painful as it was for him, he saw that he must do something, and quickly, to squelch the chatter. Somewhat stiffly, he thanked Clautz and, girding himself, headed to his own home to do what he could to repair the damage he had done, however unintentionally. He found to his dismay that Leez had no intention of making it easy for him.

He knew very well that she was not so busy that she had failed to notice his presence, but she seemed determined to pretend she had.

Realizing finally that she was not going to acknowledge him, he squatted down beside her. "It is not level."

Elise gritted her teeth but managed to refrain from making a snide remark at the observation. "I noticed."

Irritated that she seemed determined to dismiss him, Ja-rael felt his patience grow thin. "This is why I could not find the walkway in the dark. Why did you move them here?"

"You see far better than I do in the dark, so I don't believe you couldn't find the walkway. You're just looking for a reason to complain," Elise said without looking up.

"It is not nearly as convenient."

Elise finally subsided and turned to look at him. "It's prettier than harsh lines and angles--softer, more pleasing to the eye."

He frowned, looked for several moments as if he would say something and finally subsided. Elise had a feeling she knew what he'd been about to say, that she wouldn't be here that long anyway. Why would it matter to her?

She'd wondered that herself. Wryly, she wondered if it wasn't just a way of 'marking' her territory. She supposed it *was* her way of saying 'I'm here. This is me. You can ignore me, but I won't let you remain unaware that I'm here.'

After a moment, she brushed the dirt from her hands and got to her feet. Taking a hold of one of Ja-rael's wrists, she led him back to the roadway and pointed toward the inner city. "See those curling, rounded spires? Aren't they much prettier than the buildings that are flat on top?"

Ja-rael frowned. "Those with spires are many generations old. The others are newer, more--efficient."

He was right in one sense, she supposed. "Maybe, but doesn't it make you feel better, happier to be surrounded by things that you find pleasing?" she asked earnestly.

He turned to study her for what seemed an endless moment. Finally, he swallowed with some difficulty and his lips twisted in a wry smile. Instead of responding to the question, however, he turned to look at the curving walkway again. "This is more--interesting. Would you like for me to help you?"

Elise felt a smile all the way down to her toes. "Yes!"

Chapter Twenty Three

It was almost completely dark before the two of them had managed to level all of the stones. They'd worked in companionable silence for the most part, but Elise was happy enough just to feel his presence--and they couldn't argue if they didn't talk. She was tempted, more than once, to tell him her other plans for the yard. The reflection that he might object kept her from it. If he didn't know what she was planning then he couldn't accuse her of doing something he'd told her not to do.

She was tempted to offer to share the bath with him when they went inside at last, but she decided that would be pushing things too much. Instead, she suggested he take the bathroom first while she prepared the evening meal and used the sink in the cooking area for a quick, spot cleanup.

She had prepared the food and set the heat and timers for the cooking cycles by the time he came out.

He smelled so good she had to fight the urge to get closer and feast upon his scent. The fact that she was not so clean deterred her as much as her earlier reflections and she scooted past him and went in to make use of the facilities herself.

There was no sign of him when she came out and her heart failed her for several moments. Fortunately, she heard movement in the living area before she could dash to the door and embarrass herself. Content to know he was still close by, she went in to check the meal she'd prepared.

She had very little idea of what Ja-rael liked and she knew none of the dishes the Meeri prepared, but she'd learned to adapt the foods Ja-rael bought to recipes she knew and she was hopeful he would like them.

The way to a man's heart is through his stomach!

She'd begun to think she wasn't going to get the opportunity to find out if that old adage held any weight--or if it would also pertain to the Meeri male--and she was so fearful of failing at it completely and so nervous she very nearly ended up with a disaster. As it was the meat dish was underdone and the vegetable dishes she'd prepared a little overdone and she wasn't happy at all with the results.

Ja-rael didn't seem to mind. She couldn't tell that he was actually enjoying the food either, unfortunately. After studying the dishes a little doubtfully for several unnerving moments, he simply helped his plate without comment and ate.

Disappointed, Elise cast around in her mind for something to talk about that wouldn't be too inane to be interesting or too controversial. "How was your day?" she finally asked politely.

He lifted his head to look at her. His brows rose. "Uneventful."

Elise's lips twisted wryly. "I went to the market today," she said after a few moments, resisting the urge to mentally kick herself. Could she think of NOTHING interesting to say at all?

She discovered she had Ja-rael's attention. He was looking a little uneasy.

"...with Kloe, Sinata and Ania," she added quickly. "Believe me, I may not care for the customs here, but I'm not stupid and I don't have a death wish. Once was enough for me."

That comment seemed to bring up unpleasant memories. Finally, he smiled, however. "Did you buy something pretty for yourself?" he asked politely.

Elise supposed she deserved it for making such empty headed comments, but she really didn't care to be talked to as if she *was* an empty headed female who never thought about anything but clothes. "No," she mumbled, resisting the urge to tell him what she'd gone for. "But I enjoyed looking. I didn't much care for Kloe or Sinata--they're snobs--but I like Ania."

"I'm glad you are making friends."

She hadn't, not exactly anyway, but she supposed she could be friends with Ania. The only problem she could see with it was that she didn't have any more in common with Ania than she did the others. She just liked Ania better because she wasn't a mean, spiteful bitch.

She gave up on trying to hold a conversation then. She was going to have to find some common interests between them or make some by learning more about Ja-rael and his world before they would be able to talk easily about things.

He'd seemed to enjoy working with her in the yard. She was again tempted to talk to him about her plans, but once more she resisted. She was going to go stark raving mad if she didn't have something constructive to do with her time and if that something happened to be a thing Ja-rael was going to get angry about she rather thought she'd prefer to face his anger *after* she'd done what she wanted to do.

* * * *

Without really being aware of doing so, Elise found herself watching for Ja-rael the following day while she worked at laying out the beds she'd decided she was going to put in for the flowers she hoped to find. She knew he was supposed to examine Clautz's cub and she had been absently trying to think of a reasonable excuse for being there when he arrived when one abruptly popped into her mind.

She needed some sort of border to go around the beds. She could go over and re-introduce herself to Zelia and invite her to go to the market. Generally, the females always traveled as a foursome unless there was a male with them, but Elise was fairly certain Ania would be happy to go and she figured three ought to be enough. If they absolutely insisted on a fourth she would have to invite Kloe, too, but she wasn't really anxious to develop any sort of friendship with that one--even if it was possible.

After cleaning up, she headed over to the neighboring residence and rapped on the door. Zelia seemed a little taken aback by her boldness but politely invited her in. They were seated in the spacious living area struggling for conversation when Ja-rael arrived.

Elise pretended to be surprised. In point of fact, she felt downright breathless about her deception and fearful that Ja-rael would instantly figure it out. She was fairly convinced that allowing him to know how desperate she was for his attention wasn't going to get her anywhere. Anything hard to get was always far more desirable than something that just fell in one's lap like an overripe piece of fruit.

She was just about ready to do so--or seduce him--or rape him if it came to that. *He* might not be having a problem with abstinence, but she was beginning to think her brain was going to fry in its own juices.

Besides, the intimacy of sharing their bodies had been the one thing they absolutely enjoyed about each other from the first. It could be the stepping stone she needed to bring him around to the conclusion that he didn't *want* to live without her.

He checked when he saw her, but after that momentary pause, entered the room with Clautz, who'd greeted him at the door, and exchanged a few moments of pleasantries before he asked to see the child. Elise knew she was being disproportionately disappointed, but she couldn't seem to stem the feeling regardless.

He'd behaved with such excruciating politeness, though, it made her feel like a complete stranger.

She had the sense that she'd intruded when she shouldn't have.

The wail of an infant drew her from her self-absorption and she glanced at Zelia. Zelia smiled faintly. "Sadiem does not particularly care to be examined. He becomes very angry at the poking and prodding."

Elise managed a smile in return. "Who can blame the little fellow? I never much liked it myself." She studied her hands for a moment. "I suppose I should be going. I've taken up enough of your time."

"Would you like to see him?"

Elise looked up in surprise, then realized Zelia was referring to the infant.

"He is very ugly, but Ja-rael seems to think he will grow out of it and be quite handsome in time."

Elise bit her lip to keep from smiling. She was torn. Zelia didn't seem to really expect her to want to see the child, but she might be insulted if Elise expressed no interest. On the other hand, Ja-rael had already made her feel like she was trying to nose into his business. If she appeared in the nursery what other conclusion could he make?

Irritation surfaced. She wasn't going to be impolite only because she was afraid of displeasing Ja-rael. She smiled with an effort. "I'd love to!"

Zelia seemed a little disconcerted, but gestured toward the hallway that bisected the house. "It is the second room."

Elise was disconcerted then. She'd expected Zelia to escort her. Smiling again, nervously, she rose and followed the wailing down the hallway to a door that stood ajar. She could hear Ja-rael speaking softly to the infant and after nerving herself, she peered around the corner just as Ja-rael chuckled.

The sound startled her so she almost lost her balance. The sight that greeted her, however, held her transfixed. Ja-rael had just lifted the baby from its crib. "You have very good lungs, Sadiem--and a very bad temper!"

The infant continued to wail and after a moment, Ja-rael carefully placed the tiny baby against his shoulder, cupping one hand around his bobbing head and rubbing his back soothingly. "Shh, little one! I am done for today. I promise."

Elise didn't know whether to be more amazed by the way he held the infant or the fact that the infant responded to the soothing sounds of his voice and began to grow quiet. She wasn't certain how long she stood rooted to the spot as it slowly filtered through her mind why all of the children adored Ja-rael--that it was because he loved them, but it seemed an awful short time for her whole world to collapse around her. A hard knot formed in her throat. Tears pooled in her eyes.

Sensing that Ja-rael was about to turn to walk with the infant, she ducked back behind the wall and moved as quickly and quietly toward the living room as she could. Zelia merely gaped at her as she flew past the door to the living area, throwing up a hand to wave good-bye. Or perhaps it was just an impression, for she was too blinded by tears to actually see.

She didn't care either. Let Zelia think she was rude and strange.

It took every effort she could muster to keep from running as fast as she could, to force herself to maintain a sedate walk. Ja-rael's house looked impossibly far away and she had a bad feeling she wasn't going to be able to act unconcerned long enough to reach it.

She was shaking by the time she reached the house and gratefully closed the door behind her. Her chest felt so tight she had to struggle for breath. Pushing away from the door she fled to the bedroom and closed the door behind her and then pushed every piece of furniture she could move against the door.

She was hardly aware of what she was doing. All she could think of was that she could not bear to look at Ja-rael at the moment and, more importantly, she couldn't bear to have him look at her.

Dry eyed, she sat on the edge of the bed, her arms wrapped around her, rocking herself mindlessly.

How could she have been so stupid? So blind? Ja-rael had desperately wanted a mate--a mate! And all that that implied. She had been so focused on what she wanted that she'd been blind and deaf and dumb to what he'd been trying to tell her.

He couldn't make 'do' with her. She wasn't suitable at all.

Chapter Twenty Four

Elise didn't cry. It was almost worse that she discovered she couldn't, because all she could do was hold the pain inside. Up until the very moment she'd finally completely understood Ja-rael, she'd told herself that she admired him, lusted for him, respected him, even felt affection for him.

She'd lied to herself.

She loved him.

She realized something else she'd never fully understood before, too.

Love defied reason. She shouldn't feel it. She knew she shouldn't, because as sweet, and sexy and wonderful as Ja-rael was, she'd known others she could have said the same thing about and she hadn't loved them. It didn't make her hurt clear down to her soul to think about hurting them, disappointing them.

She was so very, very sorry now that she had practically slapped Ja-rael in the face with the fact that they weren't even the same species and probably couldn't reproduce. He might have figured it out eventually, but he might not have. Maybe by that time he would've loved her too much for it to matter to him--or maybe not.

She pushed those thoughts aside. She couldn't change what was already done. She couldn't even change who and what she was. What could she change? Anything? Was the situation as hopeless as it felt like it was? Or was she just too upset to think at all clearly?

The latter was certainly true, but she couldn't find the inner peace to reflect calmly. After a while she got up and began to pace the room mindlessly. She couldn't think. It was almost as if her thoughts had been so chaotic they had simply shut down and left her on autopilot.

Finally, she moved to the door and listened. When she heard nothing to suggest that Ja-rael was in the house, she returned the furniture to their original positions and went in to the facilities to take a long, hot soak. The heat of the water should have soothed her. Instead, she felt more wired when she finally managed to drag herself out.

Throwing on one of the outfits she thought of as 'everyday' wear, she went outside and tortured the yard until she was too exhausted to dig up anything else. By the time she'd bathed again she was so weary from her labors and the unaccustomed emotional upheaval that it was all she could do even to make it to the bed and collapse into blissful unconsciousness.

She was vaguely aware that Ja-rael came into the room at some point and spoke to her, but she made no attempt to surface enough to respond and he soon went away again.

By the time she woke the following day at sunrise, she'd resolved that she had been interfering in Ja-rael's life when she had no right to. She had resolved--sort of--to simply keep her distance and hope she was wrong about the way she felt about him.

Zelia had turned down the invitation for an outing saying that she was still too delicate from the birthing to consider such a long walk. At the time, Elise had simply made up her mind to ask the others, but now she found she didn't really care.

She spent most of the day trying to put the yard back the way it had been and mostly only succeeded in making it look worse. That evening, long before the time when Ja-rael might arrive, she ate a solitary meal, bathed and went into the bedroom and pushed the chest against the door.

She was still awake when he came in. She sat in the middle of the bed, listening as he moved around the house and finally arrived at her door. He pushed on it. Apparently surprised when it didn't open he hesitated for a few moments and finally tapped on the panel.

Elise held her breath and remained perfectly still. Her shoulders slumped when he left again.

The urge to cry settled like an iron weight on her chest. This time she refused even to consider giving in to it. If she did, she would be wailing worse than the infant, and Ja-rael was liable to demand to know why.

The urge vanished after a while. The weight on her chest didn't.

About halfway through the following day, while Elise was busy trying to repair the damage to Ja-rael's lawn and rehashing in her mind every single thing that had transpired between them, she suddenly recalled a dim memory that she had not fully understood at the time and had therefore carelessly discarded. The night he'd taken her, tricked her into going with him, she'd been delirious with desire for him and hadn't been able to think beyond her needs. When she'd led him to her quarters, he'd said, "I am as bound to you as you are to me. There will not be another for me."

She paused abruptly with the tool she'd been using to dig hovering in mid-air, connecting what he'd said then with something Ania had told her the day they had gone to the market.

They'd seen an elderly male selling beaded jewelry from a tiny, run down stall at one end. Ania had lingered there for some time, studying the work and had finally purchased several. Elise had thought the workmanship poor and the colors even less appealing, but she hadn't said anything.

"Poor dear old thing," Ania had murmured when they'd left.

"You know him?"

"I know of him. He lost his mate two years ago. And now he is lost and it breaks my heart."

It was sweet, but Elise wondered at so much feeling for a male she hardly knew.

"I think of my father when I see him. My mother died when I was born, you see. She was far too old to bear young, but she had been mated late in her life and she did it to please him. I asked him once when I was young why he did not find another mate. I loved him, but I wanted a mother, you see. He told me when I grew up I would understand that the Meeri males mate for life."

Elise sighed. "That's--a wonderful custom, but isn't it a little hard on those who find themselves alone?"

"It isn't just a custom for us. We are bound once we mate, heart and soul. We can not break the bounds. It isn't just that we don't wish to.

"I couldn't help but notice that you felt threatened when I spoke of Ja-rael--and I realized that it must not be the same among your people--but I am bound to Mazel. I could not break the tie if I wanted to and I have no desire to do so."

Blinking, Elise stared at the tool in her hand for several moments, wondering how long she'd been sitting in the same spot, simply staring at the trowel in her hand.

It wasn't just something Ja-rael had said in the heat of the moment, meaningless words to seduce her. Their joining had created an invisible, chemical bond that he would not be able to break and when he took her back to Tor, he would be giving up any chance for a mate and the family he wanted.

She rubbed her aching head, wondering what to do. She'd thought she would be doing what was best for him by honoring his wishes and keeping her distance. *Was* it best for him, though? Would it be better to deprive him even of companionship?

But maybe it would not be the same because she was not the same? Maybe he wouldn't be bound as he thought and he would be able to find another mate?

And maybe not. Either way, if she left without a fight, she would never know.

But was she just convincing herself that what she wanted was what was best for him?

And what of the family he wanted? If ever an individual possessed the best of qualities for becoming a parent, and deserved the chance, Ja-rael did. How much could she love him to deprive him of any possibility of it?

But would she be? The only way to know was to try.

She rejected the idea the moment it popped into her mind, but it kept coming back, like an annoying insect, buzzing around her head, disappearing for a few moments when she shooed it away and then coming right back.

She didn't know they weren't compatible breeders. Surely, either they were or they weren't and that was the only thing she need worry about?

She could try. If they weren't compatible and she wasn't impregnated, he need never know. She could leave and hope that he would have another chance.

It grew darker and darker while she sat beside the bed she'd dug and was now trying to fill back in. Finally, she got up and went inside to bathe. She never consciously made a decision. She simply disengaged her birth control devise and when she was done she set about laying a trap to seduce Ja-rael.

Chapter Twenty Five

Elise knew she was at the peak of her fertility period by the marker on her devise. If she played her cards right, she would know soon enough if there was any hope that she could make Ja-rael happy. It flitted through her mind that she was playing a dangerous game, but she ignored it. Thoughts swarmed again, teasing at her, questioning her motives and again she chased them away.

She loved Ja-rael. What she had in mind could not hurt anyone. What harm could there be in trying?

Dismissing her qualms, she bathed and scented her skin with the oils Ja-rael had bought for her. When she'd finished, she went into the bedroom and selected the most alluring of all the outfits that Ja-rael had bought for her. She'd never worn it. The robe was a deep jewel green and made of materials so fine it was almost as if she wore nothing at all. The neckline plunged deeply almost to her waist where the robe tied with a matching sash. The trousers that went with it were identical in color but a pattern of fragile vines and tiny flowers had been woven into it. When she'd finished primping, she tied a cloth over it to protect the delicate fabric from soiling and went into the cooking area to prepare a meal.

She'd just begun to think that Ja-rael would disappoint her by coming in late when she heard him at the door. Relief flooded her and at the same time her nerves drew up into a hard knot of anxiety. Her fingers shook as she quickly pulled the cloth off that she'd used to protect her clothing and hid it in a cabinet. Taking several deep, relaxing breaths, she began to set the table and set out the food she'd prepared.

She jumped guiltily when she looked up at last from her task and saw Ja-rael standing in the doorway. A wave of desire struck her like a physical blow, sending her senses reeling. Elise's hands clenched on the edge of the table while she fought the drugging dizziness and heat that washed through her. With a touch of despair she realized she could not control it, she could only be controlled by it. Without quite realizing it, she drifted toward him as if he'd summoned her.

He had. His desire was a primitive call to the primal instincts within her. She paused when she reached him, struggling to resist the urge to stroke his skin, to rub against him and feel his heat and scent engulfing her. It was important that he make the first move. She couldn't recall why, but she held onto that thought, waiting to see if he would withdraw from her again.

Uttering a deep, guttural sound, he reached for her, pulling her tightly against his length. She leaned against him, became as pliant and insubstantial as air, melted into him, blended. Her sense of self vanished as he covered her mouth with his own, became nothing more than heat, flame, tension. She caressed him as he filled her with his essence, stroking his tongue along hers in a lover's most intimate embrace, possessing the ultra sensitive flesh of her mouth. His flesh beneath her palms was heated, silky, infinitely appealing as she skated her hands along the ridge of muscle that bridged his neck and shoulder, stroked his upper arms, his back, the back of his head, traced his ears.

Coolness wafted along her shoulders as he loosened his tight hold on her and slipped his hands upward to push the shoulders of the robe down along her arms. Releasing her hold on him, she dropped her arms to allow it to fall free until she was bare to the waist. She pressed against him then, feeling the skate of the satiny fabric of his own robe, the coolness, and beneath that the hard bulge of his chest muscles, the heat of his body.

He kissed her neck, her shoulder, bent lower, tipping her over the support of one arm as he sought her breasts and teased the nipple of each until it stood erect and pouting for more attention. Abruptly, he shifted, swinging her off her feet and into his arms. Turning, he strode down the hallway into the bedroom, crossed the room and, placing a knee upon the mattress, sprawled atop its cushiony surface on top of her.

She kissed every inch of him that she could reach, enjoying the touch and taste of him on her lips and tongue as feverishly as she enjoyed his kisses. She found herself muttering his name over and over in a mindless litany. "I needed this. I needed you," she said on a gasping breath as she worked her hands beneath his robe, trying to dislodge it from his body so that nothing lay between them.

They caressed each other, undressed each other and explored every inch of flesh they exposed with the sensitive pads of fingertips, palms, lips and tongues. Elise's breath became so labored with the pounding of her heart that she swirled in and out of a heated blackness that threatened to snatch her away.

Clumsy fingers struggled with ties and fasteners, but at last they both lay completely bare, entwined, dampened by the heat of their struggles and the heat of their desire. Jarael rolled until Elise lay beneath him, stroking her breasts, molding each in turn with the palm of his hand, teasing her nipples with his fingers and his mouth and tongue until she was moaning incessantly with need. She gasped when he skated his hand along her belly and parted the folds of heated flesh between her thighs, arching up to meet his questing finger.

He dipped his head to pluck at one pert nipple as he teased her clit. She groaned, feeling her body clench. Within moments the first tremors of a climax began to spasm through her. She went rigid, gasped, cried out as he slipped his finger from her clit and along her cleft, delving inside of her. Her flesh closed around him, spasming as the echoes of release ebbed away and a new tension arose.

When he lifted his head, she scooted down, feeling his finger slip more deeply inside her with the movement. She explored his male breasts as he had explored her, teasing him with her lips and tongue and the edge of her teeth and as she did so, she slipped a palm along his hard, flat belly and cupped his sex in her hand, gently massaging the globes beneath his cock.

He groaned, tensed all over, held perfectly still as she stroked him and finally slid her palm upward and closed her fingers around his turgid flesh. He began to shake with the effort to remain still as she explored him, caressed him.

A gasp escaped him. He dragged in a shaky breath.

Abruptly, he thrust her hand away roughly. Catching her thighs, he pushed them wide and settled his hips between them, arching against her so that his cock slipped along the weeping flesh of her cleft, became slickened with the dampness of her desire for him.

Elise groaned, arched to meet him, reached for him.

He buried his face against her breasts as he levered himself upward to align his body with hers, sank the head of his cock into the mouth of her passage. Shifting, he studied her face as he slowly entered her. Sensing his gaze, Elise opened her eyes to look up at him making no attempt to hide her desire from him or her love.

That emotion intensified her pleasure in his body and their joining, rushed her upward toward culmination once more as he began to stroke her passage with the heated length of his engorged flesh. She cried out as the second wave lifted her up in a wash of ecstasy, shuddering at the intensity of the spasms that rocked her.

She heard him grit his teeth as her muscles clenched tightly around his flesh, kneaded him like clenching fingers. He paused, holding himself perfectly still as he fought for control, struggled to prolong the pleasure for both of them. After a moment, he leaned down, kissed her deeply.

She sucked his tongue greedily as he thrust it into her mouth in a rhythm that matched his possession of her nether mouth with his cock. Lifting her legs, she wrapped them around his waist, drawing his cock more deeply inside of her. He shuddered, broke the kiss abruptly and began to drive into her with desperate thrusts as he was caught up in the inescapable need to find his own glory. A thrill of renewed excitement spiraled through her at his urgency. Again, she felt the quickening, felt the rise of heat, the coiling of tension as her body rose higher and faster than before.

Heat and the dampness of his exertion radiated from his flesh as he strove, pounding faster and deeper until Elise had to hold onto him tightly to match his thrusts with a counter thrust of her own. His climax was explosive, agonizing in intensity from the growl of repletion that seemed to tear its way from his chest. It detonated a powerful reaction within her own body as it responded with harder contractions of fervent rapture.

Elise went limp with release. Ja-rael gasped, shuddered and struggled for many moments to hold his weight off of her and finally melted bonelessly against her. Despite his weight, despite the stickiness of their skin from their lovemaking, utter contentment wafted over Elise. With an effort, she lifted her arms and wrapped them around him, stroking his back lovingly, soothingly while he struggled to catch his breath. Moments passed while their hearts and breath slowed, reaching for their normal rhythms. Finally, Ja-rael disentangled himself from her arms, slipped his arms around her and rolled onto his back. Elise protested until she realized there was no way he could simply pull away and leave. When he'd settled on his back, she relaxed bonelessly on top of him.

She smiled faintly against his chest when she realized the post coital swelling peculiar to his species that had so horrified her the first time was far more welcome than she would've suspected it could be at the time. Now, she was glad because it prevented him from hit and run, allowing her to bask in the aftermath of their pleasure with one another. Now she was glad because, in her mind, she imagined his seed racing to find her own and merge with it.

The hand that had been lazily stroking her back moved upward, cupping her cheek. "A smile?" he asked huskily.

Unable to prevent a wider smile, Elise turned her face into his chest and nipped it. "You'd prefer a frown?"

He rolled onto his side, dumping her onto her side on the mattress. The tug in her nether regions told her neither of them was going anywhere, however. She draped a thigh across his hips, shifting closer, wondering it if was at all possible to arouse him again so quickly.

He studied he face for a long moment and finally sighed. "We should not have this, Elise."

Elise felt the first prick in her satisfaction. "Why not?" she asked uneasily, knowing the answer even before he said it.

"You know why."

"Tell me anyway," she heard herself say, wondering why she was so determined to make him hurt her.

"Because this will not work. Because I do not trust this devise you say will control birth and the risks are not something I want to play with."

Chapter Twenty Six

Elise lay staring at the ceiling long after Ja-rael had departed for his couch, fighting the sense of depression and inevitability, and fear, his comments had evoked.

He was not going to be happy when he discovered what she'd done.

Pushing the thought aside, she rolled out of the bed and took a long bath. When she'd dried herself and dressed again, she went in to stare glumly at the meal she'd prepared which neither of them had eaten. Sighing, she fixed herself a plate, heated it and sat down to drown her troubles.

Ja-rael, apparently having heard her, or because he was hungry, too, came in a few minutes later, fixed a plate for himself and sat down to join her. They ate in glum silence, each subject to their own fears, Elise decided, wondering if she should consider tonight a complete route or a temporary setback.

It seemed doubtful he would fall for the slinky clothing again, but she supposed it was worth a try.

The problem was he'd managed to hold out a very long time before she'd managed to catch him off guard. The likelihood was that he was going to go back to avoiding temptation by avoiding her. And, at the rate they were going, that didn't give her many more opportunities before it would be time to take her back.

Sighing, she finally decided she would spike his guns by avoiding him before he could avoid her. It seemed doubtful that tactic would work, but she couldn't think of anything else to try.

When she'd finished eating, she got up, tided the work area and, just for pure hard down meanness, turned the lights out as she left. Ja-rael sat in the dark for a good five seconds before he recovered enough from his surprise to command 'lights on' again. She slammed the door of her bedroom and for good measure, pushed the screeching, protesting trunk across the floor to barricade the door.

The prod irritated him more than she'd expected. "That is completely unnecessary," he said in a growling voice.

"Right!" she shot back at him. "Just who started it? Because it damned sure wasn't me grabbing you!"

Apparently, he didn't have an answer for that. Just as obviously, he hadn't figured out yet that the whole thing had been very carefully staged to push him over the edge.

Which was probably a good thing all things considered.

Elise spent the next day moving the walk stones back into the position she'd decided was more aesthetically appealing. As the afternoon dwindled to dusk, she went inside, bathed, fixed a solitary meal and retreated to her room.

She was still awake when Ja-rael came in and sat listening as he paced the living area, moved into the cooking area and checked the cabinets and refrigeration unit for food and finally moved back into the living area to pace some more.

He didn't come near her door.

Satisfied that she'd snubbed him first, Elise turned her lights out and went happily to sleep. The next day when she went outside to survey her new domain, she was startled to discover Ja-rael directing two young males in paving the stepping stones into a permanent slab. It would take a jackhammer to move it now and Elise retreated into the house once more until they finished and left, torn between embarrassment, amusement and irritation.

The following week when the 'ladies' made their trip to market, Elise invited herself along and, after strolling up and down the market for a while finally stopped in front of the stall that belonged to the aging male who made ugly jewelry. "These stones are pretty," she said almost idly. "I don't suppose you know where to find larger ones?"

The male tilted his head at her curiously. "How much larger?"

She showed him with her hands.

He frowned. "What would you do with such large stones?"

"I want them to form a border around a flower bed I'm making."

He scratched his head. "A bed for flowers?"

"Mmmhmm. The yard looks far too plain with only the grasses to carpet it. I want pretty plants that make bright flowers and perfume the air with their fragrance. And I want the stones to place them as a barrier so that the grasses won't choke them out."

He still looked puzzled. "What sort of flowers?"

"I don't really know--just bright colors. And I'd prefer plants that don't grow very high. If you could bring me the stones and the flowers I can pay you."

He smiled slowly. "How many do you want?"

Elise thought it over. "Do you know where the healer, Ja-rael lives?"

He nodded. "If you'll come by tomorrow, I'll show you where I mean to put them and then you'll be able to decide how many."

When they'd settled on a price per plant and per stone, she joined the others and followed them as they slowly made their way around the market and finally headed home again.

The following morning when she went out to sit on the stoop to drink her 'coffee', the old man was waiting with a rickety cart pulled by some sort of beast she'd never seen before. It seemed a placid animal, however, and she set her cup aside and crossed the lawn to see what the old man had brought her. Excitement rushed through her when she saw that he'd not only brought a pile of the stones she'd chosen, but an odd assortment of discarded containers that held a variety of plants. She studied the drooping plants while he unloaded the stones for her and finally decided to take them all.

When he'd departed, she went in the house to get water for the traumatized plants. Knowing she needed to settle them as soon as possible, she decided to focus on that task first and set the stones in place later.

It took her almost a week to complete the first bed. She spent the following week trying to coax the plants into flourishing once more. To her disappointment, some died, but she managed to save almost half and they ceased to droop dejectedly and lifted their leaves sunward.

Heartened by her success, she went to the market the following week and asked the old man to bring her more flowers.

The exercise was salve to her wounds, but she discovered it went deeper than that once she'd finally completed the bed and sat back to admire it. It brought back such sweet

memories of home--of Earth--that it made her happy and
sad all at the same time.

When she sat on the stoop, drinking the hot brew, basking
in the morning sun and the cool air, she could almost
imagine that she *was* on Earth once more, staring at her
own yard.

She was so enthralled with it that she hardly noticed that
Ja-rael had returned until his shadow fell across her. She
looked up at him then, surprised to find that he'd returned
to the house when he could not have been gone more than a
few hours. To her embarrassment, she discovered tears had
filled her eyes as she sat staring at the flowers. When she
blinked, they ran down her cheeks. She chuckled self-
consciously as she wiped the moisture away. "It reminds
me of home. I've spent the past two years trying not to
think of Earth at all, and now I find I've spent the past
several weeks trying to …." She broke off abruptly. "Sorry.
I guess I'm blocking you," she said, jumping to her feet as
it suddenly occurred to her that she was sitting in the
middle of the steps.

He studied her for several moments, then, instead of
moving past her, he pulled her against his length in a tight
embrace. "I am so sorry, meesha. If it makes you happy,
you may transform my entire yard as you please. I will even
help you if you like."

Elise chuckled, but shook her head as she pulled away.
"You have far too many important things to do. And--I
need to do this myself."

He looked almost disappointed, but merely nodded and
left her on the stoop as he went inside, collected the things
he needed and departed once more.

Elise sighed as she watched him go. He *was* a good
hearted man. Despite their differences, despite all the little
things she'd done for weeks with no other objective in
mind than to tease him unmercifully, he had seemed to
sense that she needed the comfort of an embrace at that
moment without any pressure for anything more. And he'd
given her what she needed without hesitation, as if it was
the most natural thing in the world and something he did
every day.

The sense of comfort slowly dissipated as she sat again to
stare at the tiny piece of home she'd captured in her little

flower bed. After a time it dawned upon her that Ja-rael had never, in all the time she'd known him, 'forgotten' anything.

He'd come home to see her.

* * * *

Elise didn't know whether to be more excited, or more terrified when she realized her plan had worked. Her first reaction was disbelief and she realized that, in the back of her mind, she hadn't really expected it to be possible, especially not on the first try. And she hadn't been certain she would get the chance of a second try. The shocked disbelief hadn't worn off when excitement began to take hold. She spent a week smiling to herself and fighting the urge to tell Ja-rael right away, imagining all sorts of thrilling scenarios about his reaction to her wonderful news.

She might not have been able to resist the urge to break the news as soon as possible except that she remained in a state of disbelief herself for so long and the fear tormented her that it was just a fluke. Either she would find that she'd been mistaken, or, worse, it would transpire that the seed hadn't taken firm root, or something wasn't as it should be and she the fetus would abort.

The only way she could keep her news to herself was to continue to avoid Ja-rael as much as possible, because whenever she was around him the urge to tell him was nearly overwhelming. Ja-rael made it easy for her since he was trying to avoid temptation and Elise focused on transforming the yard to as close an approximation of the tiny yard she recalled from her childhood home on Earth as she could.

By the time it had thoroughly sank in that she really was breeding and that the fetus had dug in with every intention of staying, her thrill about her condition had ebbed enough for some very sobering thoughts to sink in.

First and foremost was the fact that Ja-rael seemed to have made up his mind that, regardless of his desire to have a family, the risks of trying to have one with Elise were not something he was willing to accept. And Elise knew by this time how stubborn Ja-rael could be once he made up his mind.

He'd concluded almost the moment they'd arrived on Meeri that a mating between them was not possible and nothing she'd done in the months since had budged him one iota. If anything truly set him apart from his human counterpart, Elise thought it was that one grim determination even to avoid sexual intimacy with her. Of course she knew the reason he wouldn't was because he feared impregnating her, but she was fairly certain there wasn't a human male in the universe that would be able to remain stubbornly abstinent when they had a willing, even eager, female right under their nose--even if they didn't especially *want* that particular female. And she was fairly certain that wasn't the case with Ja-rael. He might not love her. He might not even desire her as he had to begin with when he'd been laboring under the impression that she was his kind, but he still wanted her.

She felt it. As hard as he worked to keep his libido in check, she was so finely attuned to his pheromones that even a little slip that allowed a minute amount of pheromones to be released in his bloodstream was enough to send a wave of responding need through her--even if she happened to be in another room with a barricaded door between them.

She continued to barricade the door, not because she thought there was any danger at all of him trying to come in, but because she knew it annoyed the hell out of him. That changed when she finally arrived at the realization that, far from being overjoyed at her news, Ja-rael was much more likely to be horrified and/or furious that she'd deliberately done the one thing he feared most--risked a pregnancy when neither of them knew what the outcome might be.

Chapter Twenty Seven

Ja-rael's resolve didn't sustain him nearly as long as Elise had expected, and begun to hope, it would. Just about the time she realized with alarm that she was running out of time for breaking the news to him gently, his resolve crumbled like so much dust.

He'd begun to arrive home earlier and earlier and Elise had only narrowly managed to retreat to her room and barricade the door on several occasions. That fact seemed to goad him, for he began to prowl the hallway, pacing back and forth past her door.

Then, the one thing Elise hadn't counted on happened. She had to pee. She tried to ignore it, but the growth of her womb had begun pressing down on her bladder and she found she had to go--or at least felt like she had to go--more and more frequently. When Ja-rael finally ceased to pace back and forth in front of her door, she moved to the chest and eased it away from the door as quietly as possible, flinching when the thing protested.

Pausing, she listened for several moments and finally opened the door quietly and tiptoed to the facilities. When she emerged, Ja-rael was standing in the hallway outside, one shoulder propped against the wall, his arms crossed. She jumped guiltily, her eyes widening in surprise.

Desire hit her with such force it squeezed the air from her lungs. One moment she was gaping at him, the next she was enveloped in a haze of passion that swept every thought from her mind and left only need. Their passage from the hallway to the bedroom became a struggle to disentangle themselves from their clothing without yielding the need to touch, to caress each other. They fell into the bed half clothed, trapped by the clothing that had tangled around them and become frustrating bindings. Elise, who wore nothing more than a robe for sleeping, had her elbows bound to her waist and couldn't seem to wiggle free. She ceased trying when Ja-rael tossed the hem of her robe over her face and buried his face in her mound. For several moments the sensation was so exquisite she thought she would faint. A tiny climax erupted through her almost the moment she felt the faint roughness of his tongue glide over her clit. She shuddered, bucked against him and began to thrash frantically as the spasms increased in intensity instead of dissipating. Uttering a growl, he planted his hands on her arms and held her down, licking and sucking and teasing her clit until her body convulsed in a harder spasm of release and she began to beg him to stop before she died of lack of oxygen, for she could not seem to drag in enough air.

He lifted his head finally, sat up on his knees. Reaching for her, he dragged her toward him, lifting her onto his lap and thrusting into her at almost the same moment. She gasped, caught his shoulders to balance herself as he held her hips, delving deeper and deeper inside her in a series of short thrusts until he his cock was so deep inside of her she felt the head of his cock against her womb. He set the rhythm then, lifting her hips and then pushing down again until he filled her before he lifted her again with agonizing slowness.

Dizzily, Elise followed his silent command, feeling her body sheathe his hard flesh until her heart was pounding with excitement and then the slow, wondrous caress of his flesh along hers as he retreated. The tension grew in her again. Her body, rising toward another release, rapidly reached the peak. She began to move faster, bear down on him harder as she teetered on the brink. When it broke, the spasms were so hard she found it almost impossible to maintain the rhythm she'd set. Abruptly, Ja-rael tipped her onto her back and took control, thrusting into her with a savage possession that made her body peak twice, convulse with nearly unbearable rapture. She was still gasping weakly with her release when he began to shudder and quake with his own culmination. Wrapping her arms around him, she held him tightly to her, relishing the tremors of pleasure she felt go through him.

When at last they lay beside one another, panting in repletion, she snuggled close, resisting the temptation to confess her love for him by showing it instead with her caresses.

She was drifting toward sleep when Ja-rael pulled away from her at last. His hand came to rest on her rounded belly for several moments.

"Leez, what have you done?"

Elise was suddenly wide awake. Try as she might, her mind instantly leapt to the hand resting on her belly and from there to her perfidy and guilt flooded her cheeks with color. "What do you mean?" she asked evasively.

He frowned with a mixture of dawning anger and uneasiness. Sitting up, he fit his hand more firmly over her belly. Elise sat up as well, thrusting his hand off. He stared at her tight lipped for several moments and finally pushed her back against the bed, daring her with a hard look to defy him.

Elise lapsed into fuming silence, not because she was afraid to defy him but because she had realized that there was no point at all in trying to keep the secret any longer. Her belly was already noticeably swollen. At the rate she was going she couldn't have kept it from him more than a few weeks anyway.

When he saw she had no intention of further struggle, he placed both hands on her belly and gently pressed his fingers into her flesh just above her pubic bone. Feeling around with his other hand, the found the upper edge of her womb and measured it.

He sat back on his heels abruptly, his face leached of color. "You're breeding."

Elise considered pretending surprise. She realized fairly quickly, though, that she wasn't likely to convince him. "I'd wondered...," she said vaguely.

His eyes narrowed. "You did not wonder. You knew. And you knew because you planned this! Why? Why would you do such a thing? Take such a terrible risk?"

Elise eyed him petulantly. She sure as hell wasn't going to tell him that it was because she loved him so desperately she couldn't think of anything else to try to hold onto him-- not when he was glaring at her so accusingly.

"Because I didn't want to go back to that horribly miserable place and you were determined to take me!" she snapped.

He looked at her like he'd never seen her before. Elise felt a horrible sinking sensation in her chest as he withdrew from her, moved away, and finally sat on the edge of the bed, his back to her.

Belatedly, Elise realized she had said the wrong thing. She should have swallowed her pride and told him it was because she loved him, even if he was angry. She should have told him it was because she loved him so much that she couldn't bear to think of depriving him of the children he wanted so badly. What she had said was probably the worst thing she could possibly have thought of to say because it made it sound as if her motives had been totally selfish, that she was so focused on her comfort that nothing else really mattered to her.

After several uncomfortable moments, she sat up and leaned toward him to caress his back. "I love you," she said tentatively.

He pulled away from her and stood up. "You gave no thought at all to the innocent whose life and health you were risking?"

Elise gaped at him at the accusation, too stunned for several moments even to think of a response. "I didn't!" she protested. "It wasn't like that at all! I know we're different, but I figured it would either take or it wouldn't. You see it's growing just fine."

"I do not see anything but that you have a mixed breed in your belly. *You* do not know it is fine. *I* do not know. And because you kept this from me you are too far along now to do anything about it even if the cub is--not right."

Elise felt her chin wobble, but resolutely dismissed his horrible suggestion that the child might be abnormal. "I'm not that far along. I haven't even known it myself but a few weeks."

"You are in your second trimester."

Elise's jaw dropped in stunned surprise. "I can't be! I didn't disengage the birth control more than two months ago, in the first place. In the second, *that* was the first time you'd touched me in months!"

Ja-rael stared at her, stunned.

Uneasiness began to grow in Elise at the expressions she saw chase each other across his face as he mentally calculated. "What's wrong?"

Ja-rael looked away from her. Finally, he merely shook his head. "I don't know that anything is. Tomorrow--when I am not so angry--I will check you."

Elise settled back when he'd left. Her emotions were in turmoil, however, and she didn't know which was uppermost, fear or grief. Ja-rael hadn't even responded when she'd told him she loved him, most likely because he hadn't believed her. Of all the stupid things she could've done, that probably ranked highest. The fear that he'd been withholding something from her refused to rest either and she slept little.

Ja-rael woke her the following morning by appearing at her bedside with his bag. Without a word, he began examining her. Elise was too depressed and too weary to protest and merely did whatever he asked. Finally, frowning thoughtfully, he returned his instruments to his bag.

"Well?" Elise asked uneasily when he said nothing.

He forced a faint smile that she supposed was to reassure her. Somehow, it didn't, perhaps because he didn't look as if he'd gotten any more sleep than she had--and he looked worried.

"You seem healthy."

Elise eyed him irritably. "I *know* I'm healthy. What about the baby?"

His smile wavered. "I'll have to study the data I've collected."

* * * *

Elise had suspected, of course, that Ja-rael was making excuses to be gone most of the time, but it wasn't until he discovered she was pregnant that she became certain she'd been right. He was still gone a great deal of the time, but he managed to make it home at least once in the course of each day and usually more than once. Elise might have been gratified by the attention except that he looked more haggard with worry every time he checked her. No matter how hard he tried to hide it from her, she knew he was worried sick, that he couldn't sleep, could hardly eat, and it scared the pure hell out of her.

Equally scary was the fact that the baby seemed to be growing at an unnerving rate. She had never born a child before, but she had certainly seen it done and she couldn't recall that anyone else had ballooned as she was. Whenever she asked him about the baby, though, he would only say that it seemed strong and healthy. When she asked him if it didn't seem to him that it was growing awfully fast, he would just give her a sickly smile and tell her it looked like it might be a big baby.

Elise had begun to wonder if it was a baby at all. Just about the time she became convinced that she had a horrible tumor growing inside of her instead of a beautiful baby, however, she felt the first flutters of movement. Ja-rael looked marginally relieved at the announcement, but only a little.

One day, when she was by her calculations about half way through her term and already so big she was having trouble reaching her feet, he came home early and announced that he was going to take her to see a friend of his in Tylina, the capitol city of the Meeri nation. Elise had mixed feelings about it. She was uncomfortable most of the time. As thrilling as the idea of a trip was, she didn't particularly relish taking a long trip in Ja-rael's glider.

He soothed her fears, telling her that Clautz was going to give them a lift to the shuttle, which they would be taking to Tylina.

Elise wasn't entirely certain of what he meant, but decided it must be some sort of transit system. She discovered she'd been correct. Even better, Clautz was far better at landing than Ja-rael and his vehicle much more comfortable.

She supposed she had realized that Modun, where they lived, couldn't possibly be the only city the Meeri boasted, but she was still surprised as the shuttle settled in a string of towns from small hamlets to cities nearly as large as Modun to disgorge passengers and take on more. Despite their early departure, it was nearing dusk when they finally saw the lights of the city of Tylina.

Elise had spent most of the trip with her nose stuck to the viewing panel, drinking in the sights and sounds of a world vital with life. Homesickness swept over her with the memories it evoked of Earth, but it was more a gentle sadness than a great sorrow. Earth was gone, but Meeri--Meeri was like coming home again. It was green, and beautiful, and bustling with the labors of those who worked to support the civilization that supported them--just as Earth had once been.

Gasping at the sheer enormity of the city they were approaching, Elise finally turned wide, excited eyes toward Ja-rael. "It's huge!" she whispered in awe.

He smiled faintly. "It is--which is why I prefer to live in Modun. This is where I trained as a healer."

Elise's brows rose questioningly. "And this friend you've come to see--he studied with you?"

Ja-rael's smile wavered. "Tania was my teacher." He took her hand. "I want him to look at you. He knows more than any other. If –anything is amiss, he will be able to tell us."

Elise felt her pleasure vanish. It wasn't as if she hadn't suspected he had a particular reason for wanting to go. She'd even thought it was possible that she was the reason, but she'd hoped that wasn't it at all. She'd hoped that it was simply business that took Ja-rael to Tylina and he hadn't wanted to leave her behind.

She should have known better, she thought glumly, girding herself for yet another unpleasant examination.

Chapter Twenty Eight

Tania came as a complete surprise. He looked scarcely older than Ja-rael, although Elise was obliged to admit that it was a little difficult to determine Ja-rael's age as far as that went. Regardless, since he was Ja-rael's teacher, she reasoned, he must be a good bit older than he looked.

Beyond that, he was the first boisterously out-going Meeri she'd met. The moment they entered his office, he surged forward with an exuberant step, grinning widely. "Ja-rael! I have not seen you in ages! And this must be Leez, your mate you were telling me about?"

Elise flinched as he patted her swollen belly affectionately, but he'd withdrawn his hand before she even realized his intention.

"And this little fellow looks to be coming along nicely."

Elise glanced up at Ja-rael at that and he forced a smile. "Yes. But I will feel better once you have examined her. We are anxious."

"As two new parents would be," Tania agreed, ushering the two of them from the reception area and into another room that turned out to be an office rather than the examining room Elise was dreading. When they were seated, Tania settled behind the desk and beamed at the two of them. "How may I help?"

Ja-rael frowned. "Did you not get the message I sent you?"

Tania scratched his head thoughtfully a moment. "Yes! Indeed, I did. And your concern is…?"

Ja-rael looked nonplused. He cleared his throat, glanced at Elise uncomfortably and finally spoke. "She is not--Meeri."

Tania nodded.

Ja-rael finally sat forward. "We are different."

Tania chuckled. "Indeed! She is a tribute to her race--a lovely creature. You are a lucky man, Ja-rael, to have such a beautiful female to bear you companionship and bear your children."

Ja-rael flushed. "I know this and I am deeply grateful. However, I am concerned that there could be complications."

Tania shook his head dismissively. "I understand why you would be concerned, but she is the picture of health--at least, she appears to be to me. I have never seen the like of her before, but she appears strong and healthy. The babe is growing quite nicely."

Again, Ja-rael shifted uneasily. "But, sir, she is only halfway through her term."

Tania's brows rose. He studied the mound of Elise's belly for several moments and finally got to his feet. "We'll just have a look, shall we?"

The moment Elise had been dreading had arrived. She was sent to remove her clothing while Ja-rael spoke with Tania. When she emerged from the dressing room a few minutes later, clutching a sheet to herself, the two of them were still deep in conversation. She shifted uneasily from one foot to the other, studying the examination room. It looked remarkably like those she was familiar with, but she supposed it only stood to reason it would. They were both humanoid races.

Finally Ja-rael noticed her presence. Breaking off his conversation with Tania, he strode toward her and helped her onto the examination table.

He didn't depart, which Elise found disconcerting, particularly since she was the only one in the room naked. He did retreat a short distance, however.

As Ja-rael generally did, Tania examined her first with his eyes and his hands. When he'd finished, he stepped away to pick up an instrument and placed one end in his ear. The other, he placed upon her abdomen, moving it to one spot, pausing, then moving it again. Finally, he removed the instrument, studied her for several moments and approached Ja-rael.

Elise strained to hear what they were saying but both spoke in low voices and she could only catch a word here and there.

"Is there something wrong with its heart?" she demanded when Tania and Ja-rael both approached her and began to move some sort of scanning devise into position above her.

Tania's smile was a little forced. "We're going to find out."

Elise did her best not to allow her imagination to terrorize her but when they had turned on the scanning devise and both of them simply stared at the screen, transfixed, she began to get very scared. "What is it?"

"Two," Ja-rael said as if he'd never heard the word before, then glanced at her face. "Two."

"Two what?" Elise demanded, more frightened still by the look of panic on Ja-rael's face.

"This is--unprecedented," Tania breathed in awe.

"What?" Elise demanded.

"If I wasn't seeing it with my own eyes, I would never believe it."

"Goddamnit to hell!" Elise yelled at them. "Tell me!"

"Two," Ja-rael repeated, apparently unable to formulate any other words at the moment.

"Give me that damned scanner!" Elise growled, sitting up abruptly and turning it so that she could see the screen. She didn't know what she'd expected, but the image on the screen was startlingly clear as if the muscle and tissue that separated her from seeing within her womb were virtually transparent. A thrill of joy went through her. "They're beautiful! I should have known it was twins, the way they were growing--and the activity. Believe me it feels like the two of them are playing soccer with my organs."

"Twins?" Ja-rael repeated, examining the unfamiliar word.

Elise giggled. "Yes! Twins! Who'd have thought--and girls! You don't mind do you, Ja-rael?"

"Mind?"

Elise frowned at him. "What is wrong with you? You knew I was pregnant!"

"But two," he said again.

"That's what twins are--two."

It finally sank in on him that she wasn't nearly as surprised as he was. "This is something you know?"

Elise was puzzled. "Having twins?" she finally asked cautiously.

"You have a word for it," he said with sudden incite.

Elise nodded. "Twins for two, Triplets for three, Quadruplets for four, Quintuplets for five, and Septuplets, I think, for six."

Tania and Ja-rael exchanged a look of disbelief. Tania laughed. "Now you are teasing."

Elise frowned. "No, I'm not."

"Your people have--liters?" Ja-rael demanded, aghast. "No wonder your world had population problems!"

Elise glared at him. "I told you we could have multiple births, but we damned sure don't have liters! Twins are fairly common, but the others are fairly rare. It does happen occasionally. The reason I'm not that surprised is because I'm genetically likely to have them. It runs in my family." She frowned as a thought occurred to her. "God! I hope the next isn't quads."

Ja-rael was strangely subdued as they left Tania's office and went to find a room for the night. As accustomed as Elise was to his reticence, she noticed it was more than that and when they'd finally settled for the evening she began to prod him to try to find out what was wrong.

"Did Tania find anything wrong?"

Ja-rael stared at her for a full minute before he spoke. "Besides the twins?"

Elise was offended. "You're not happy that it's twins?" she asked tightly.

He looked torn. "I have never been more terrified by anything in my life. I don't know anything about twins--nothing. I don't think any Meeri has ever had two at once."

Elise settled beside him on the bed. "I'll be fine, Ja-rael. It's not that much different."

He nodded, but he didn't look relieved or the least bit reassured.

To her great disappointment, although they shared a bed, Ja-rael was too distant to share his body with her. Sighing, Elise turned her back to him, shifted until she found a reasonably comfortable position and finally went to sleep.

If anything, Ja-rael looked worse the following morning and Elise suspected he hadn't slept at all. When she fussed over him, however, he snarled at her, apologized profusely and thereafter gave her the cold shoulder.

It was barely daylight when they boarded the shuttle again for the flight back to Modun. As weary as Elise was, she noticed the stares. She should've been used to it by now. She couldn't go anywhere on Meeri without having small fingers pointed in her direction and curious, but embarrassed adult stares. Whispering had been added to the stunned stares, however. At first, Elise thought she was imagining it, but each time the shuttle stopped to take on passengers, they would stare at her all the way by and then the excited whispers would begin again.

Ja-rael seemed oblivious to it, though, and after a while Elise finally decided her imagination was running away with her.

It wasn't. When they reached Modun, the terminal was clogged with people.

"I wonder what's going on?" Elise asked, nudging Ja-rael. "This isn't usual, is it?"

Ja-rael stared at the throng as if just awaking from a dream. Finally, he frowned in puzzlement. "This is not usual, no. I can not imagine what is happening."

They weren't left in the dark long. The moment they emerged from the shuttle someone screamed, "There she is. That's her!"

Elise glanced around sharply, but saw no one.

Ja-rael's hand tightened on her arm. "Mother of Meeri!" Ja-rael ground out the curse. "They know!"

"Know what?" Elise gasped as he dragged her quickly around the side of the shuttle, glanced frantically from side to side in search of something and then swept her into his arms and began to run with her.

Under the circumstances, it was impossible to talk, but Elise was growing more and more alarmed as she saw the Meeri begin to surge around the shuttle behind them. Ja-rael rounded a corner and the mob disappeared from view. Spying an exit sign, he raced toward it, snatched the door open and then set her down long enough to disable the door by ripping the handle off.

"What's going on?"

"They know about the twins--maybe even that you are not Meeri. I don't know. Tania did not seem to believe that part, but he obviously could not keep the news of the twins to himself," he said absently, grabbing her hand and leading her down the stairs to a second door. When they emerged,

Elise saw that they were near a wooded area. After glancing around again, Ja-rael led her into the woods.

"This is about the twins?" Elise gasped, completely stunned.

Ja-rael gave her a look. "We Meeri do not have twins. We rarely have two at all, let alone together. You have not noticed this for yourself?"

Elise felt real fear for the first time. "What will they do to me if they catch us?"

Ja-rael shook his head. Dragging her toward him, he kissed her hard on the mouth. "I do not intend to find out." He shook his head at the look on her face. "I think they are only excited, but it is a mob. They could hurt you without intending to."

He dragged her quickly deeper and deeper into the wooded area. When he saw that she was holding her side, he swept her into his arms and carried her a while. Finally, he stopped near a like trickle of water that was more of a ditch than a stream, settled her on the ground and looked her over keenly. "You are alright?"

Elise nodded. "As well as can be expected considering I've just been scared out of ten years of life."

Ja-rael looked alarmed.

"It's just an expression. What are we going to do?"

Ja-rael thought it over for some time. Finally, he looked at her apologetically. "I expect the excitement will die down with time. I'm worried about the 'until then' part. I think I must take you to stay in my ship until the cubs are born."

"Alone?" Elise asked weakly.

Ja-rael caught her face between his hands. "How could you think that, meesha?"

She studied his earnest expression for several moments and finally relaxed. "I don't mind."

"I do," Ja-rael said wryly, "but I can think of no other way to keep you safe. For now, as much as I hate to, I must leave you alone for a little while."

Elise felt a knot form in her throat, but she didn't argue.

He shook his head. "I must get things that I will need to care for you. I'll need to get the glider, too. You can't run. I don't want to take a chance that you would get hurt."

It made perfect sense, of course, and she still didn't like the idea of being left alone. Regardless, she knew she would only be wasting time to argue. "I understand."

He swallowed audibly. "I don't believe they will follow, but they will recognize my scent. Yours--I don't think they will. I want you to follow this steam in that direction until you are near the clearing on the other side. I will meet you there in an hour with the glider."

Elise's chin wobbled. "I'll get lost. You know I have a terrible sense of direction."

"Walk in the stream. If the water peters out, stay in the hollow it has formed. You won't get lost. I won't let you."

Elise wasn't happy about it, but finally she struggled to her feet with Ja-rael's help and stepped into the water carefully. It was cold and a shiver went through her. Forcing a tight smile for Ja-rael's benefit, she turned and started to walk carefully along the streambed. When she looked around again, Ja-rael had vanished from sight.

Chapter Twenty Nine

After fleeing for their lives, the uneventful trip from Mordun to the site where Ja-rael kept his ship was almost a let down. True to his word, Elise heard Ja-rael's glider settle in the clearing at the edge of the woods only a little over an hour later, but it was nearly dark by the time Elise finally managed to make her way through the woods and nothing short of a miracle that she'd done so without getting lost. She was so relieved to see Ja-rael when he came racing toward her in the woods that she promptly burst into tears. Ja-rael was immediately convinced that something terrible had happened and insisted upon examining her despite her protests. When he'd assured himself that she wasn't hurt, he carried her to the glider and settled her inside with great care before climbing in himself. The flight took just over an hour and a half, but it was already dark by the time they landed in the small clearing Ja-rael had used before and they were still miles from the ship.

Elise had braced herself for the landing, but Ja-rael exercised patience for once and took the vehicle in slowly to keep from jarring her. Relieved, she smiled at him. "That wasn't bad at all. What now?"

Ja-rael brushed the backs of his fingers along her cheek in an affectionate caress. "I carry you as I did before."

Elise looked at him a little doubtfully. "I'm heavier and rounder than before," she pointed out.

He chuckled, caressing her belly. "I will manage. I mean for you to have a bed to sleep in tonight."

They waited until the moons had risen to leave. With their light Elise could see almost well enough to walk herself. Although he made it clear he wasn't happy about it, Ja-rael allowed her to have her way until she began to grow tired. When she asked to stop and rest, he swept her into his arms and carried her the remainder of the way.

The ship seemed more cramped than ever, particularly after all the time Elise had spent in the comfortable little house that Ja-rael owned, but she was glad for the chance of a bed all the same. It made it all the more delightful that Ja-rael, after securing the hatch, climbed into bed beside her and curled close against her back. Elise smiled sleepily as his arm settled over her. "This is nice. It will be the first time we ever shared a bed to sleep."

Ja-rael spent most of the following week working on making their 'nest' comfortable, which primarily consisted of thoroughly cleaning the hold which smelled none too lovely from the animals that had been there. When he'd thoroughly cleaned it and aired it, he began working on the hatch and gangplank, devising and installing a simple security bar.

That task made Elise uneasy, but she discovered her fears were groundless. Ja-rael never left her for more than a few hours at the time--which made her wonder where he was getting the supplies he kept returning with. When she finally asked, he told her he had worked out a rendezvous point with Clautz who would gather the things he requested and bring them. All Ja-rael then had to do was meet him at the pickup point.

Elise didn't think too much about Ja-rael's practice until she realized that they had been 'camping' for nearly two months and Ja-rael had not so much as mentioned the need to leave to see about them. As loathe as she was to broach the subject, she finally asked him one evening while they were sitting around the campfire Ja-rael had built for them in the clearing.

He merely shrugged. "I made arrangements with the other healers to take care of them until we get back. You are by far the most important of my patients."

Elise, who was sitting between his legs and using his chest as a backrest, glanced around at him. "You did? Aren't you worried that you won't have any patients when you get back?"

"No."

She frowned in surprise, but decided not to pursue it. Instead, she settled comfortably once more, staring up at the night sky. "What is that?" she asked after a time, pointing to a bright dot in the sky larger than all the others.

Ja-rael was silent for so long that she thought he would tell her he didn't know. "Tor," he said finally. "It grows nearer as it does each year around this time."

"Oh," Elise responded, wishing she hadn't asked.

Tightening his arms around her, Ja-rael dipped his head and kissed her neck, then placed his cheek against hers. "I know that I made a promise to you, Leez, and I have been an abominable mate, but you said that you had changed your mind. Will you stay with me?"

It took a strenuous effort to keep from bursting into tears and all she could do to speak around the painful knot that formed in her throat. "I was afraid you wouldn't ask," she managed to say finally. She lifted a hand to stroke his cheek. "When I said I didn't want to go back because I hated it on Tor--well, it's true, but that's not the real reason I wanted to stay, and it certainly isn't the reason I wanted to have your baby."

"You wanted to have my baby?" Ja-rael asked, his voice sounding strangely hoarse.

Elise drew a shuddering breath. "When I saw you that day with Zelia's infant I knew I loved you and it hurt so much to think I might not be able to give you the family you wanted that I knew I had to try. I realize now that it was a terribly irresponsible thing to do, but I wasn't thinking very clearly just then."

He shifted, touching her cheek and making her look at him. "Do you, love me?"

"With all my heart."

A slow smile curled his lips. "Even though I'm--not of your race?"

Elise smiled. "I'm not sure love recognizes race. It's too-- deep to have anything to do with any concept of the mind. It just happens. It just *is*."

His gaze flickered over her face. "I can not tell you how deeply I regret the time I squandered when I could have been with you. It was...." He paused. "I could not think very clearly."

"You're with me now."

"But I can't get back what I threw away."

Elise studied him a long moment and finally struggled to get to her feet. Puzzled, Ja-rael helped her up. She grasped his hand then, leading him toward the gangplank.

"What are you up to?" he asked, chuckling.

"Making up for lost time."

Laughing, Ja-rael pulled her to a halt when they'd reached the top of the gangplank. "We should not."

"Don't start that again!"

"The twins?"

"Can complain about it later. When they get here we're really going to have a lot of time to make up for." She paused. "Unless--you don't want to?"

He gave her a look and a wall of desire crashed over her.

* * * *

The twins arrived early. Elise had known they very likely would, but she had decided that there was no point in alarming Ja-rael unnecessarily, particularly when there was nothing either of them could do about it. He was already uneasy about attending his first multiple birth. Most likely he would have been anyway, but his anxiety was compounded by the fact that they were his.

Despite his fears and her inexperience, the birthing was straightforward and without complication--almost a month ahead of schedule, but otherwise completely unremarkable.

Elise didn't have time to anticipate birth pains, which she thought was just as well since she would have been tensed against it otherwise. As babies so often do, she went into labor at the most inconvenient time--just as they were going to bed--and arrived just at daybreak, but in the interim, Ja-rael finally showed her why he was referred to as a healer, rather than a physician. He controlled her pain, muted it to a bearable level without any need at all for drugs of any kind, merely by touching her.

When both had arrived, Ja-rael very carefully lay the squalling infants side by side on the mattress so that they could study and admire them. A strangeness washed over Elise as she studied her infants--a sense of alienation, for they bore the markings and coloration of their father. Concern touched her and she wondered why it felt strange to her when Ja-rael felt as completely right to her as her own body.

Curiously, she examined them with her hand, uncurling tiny fingers to count them, studying the tiny toes. Finally, she scooped the one nearest her up in her arms and cradled it to her chest. At once its wails began to subside and within moments it was snuffling hungrily at her chest in search of dinner. Bemused, Elise looked up at Ja-rael and discovered that he'd cradled the other infant just as she had and suddenly it felt just exactly right.

Rubbing a hand over the baby's head, she kissed the delicate skin of her forehead and then held her away to study her. The baby squinted at her and she chuckled at its efforts to adjust its vision to the sudden brightness of the world, the look of wonder on its tiny face.

The babies had her eyes, her chin, and her hair.

She looked up at Ja-rael on a sudden thought. "I just realized something."

"What?"

"You have two maned lionesses, Ja-rael!"

Epilogue

Kathryn paused in her hoeing and placed a hand on her aching back, arching against it to stretch her cramping muscles. Around her, the other women continued to work the lush garden their little community shared. They were a pitiful lot. Three years earlier the ship that had carried them safely across the known universe from Earth to their new world had ended it's voyage by crashing into the planet and killing more than half the passengers. Everyone had lost someone. Some entire families had been wiped out.

At first, they had simply been so stunned by the magnitude of the disaster and their personal losses no one had really assessed the true scope of the devastation.

It had begun to sink in upon them when they'd been forced to set aside their grief and plunge immediately into the work of establishing a colony before they lost any more colonists. The dead and dying had drawn predators from the jungle because there hadn't been enough living left to tend the injured and bury the dead quickly enough. In the end, they hadn't been able to bury them at all. They'd had to form a mass funeral pyre and burn the bodies to keep the wildlife from carrying off anyone else.

It was when they began to build their first crude shelters that they discovered that, while overall they'd lost little more than half the colonists, the ratio of men to women was far worse. Unfortunately, as bad as it was, it got worse. Over the next three years the men had dwindled until there were only a handful over the age of fifteen and under the age of sixty. They'd lost two entire hunting parties the first year. Six men had left the compound in search of meat, none had come back.

It was pretty hopeless for them now and they couldn't even really call what they had a colony anymore. They were just survivors and for most of the women, like her, that was all they were ever going to be--survivors. Even if every single male who was capable of producing a family chose a wife, that would still leave nearly thirty women with no male at all, and no hope of a family. Everyone knew it, but no one admitted it out loud.

They'd become so fearful of losing what little they had left that the women had finally assumed the role of hunter and protector--and they'd begun fighting over the men that were left, as undesirable as most of them would've been if there'd been an alternative.

Sighing, Kathryn flicked a resentful glance at the men sprawled in the shade of the trees at the edge of the field. Supposedly, they were standing guard. In reality they were doing what they usually did--nothing. As she watched, Brad, the true prima donna of the group because he was the 'prime' male, lifted a hand lazily and summoned one of the women working nearby to fetch him a drink.

Grinding her teeth, Kathryn went back to hoeing. She'd been hoeing furiously for all of ten minutes when a strange sensation washed over her. She paused, trying to brace herself on the hoe as a wave of dizziness followed it.

God help her, was she coming down with something?

Heat stroke?

She felt really warm. A strange scent or taste filled her.

Seizure?

She looked up, wondering if she should call for help. As she scanned the field around her her attention was caught by movement at the edge of the field. Terror instantly warred with the other sensations that were growing steadily worse when she saw they were being stalked by predators.

As if he realized he'd been spotted, one of the predators paused. After a moment, he stood up and Kathryn felt her jaw go slack with surprise. It stood on two legs. It was as tall as a man--it was a man--sort of. He was wearing what looked to be a loincloth, a sure sign that this was no animal at all, but an intelligent species.

Their gazes locked across the space that separated them and Kathryn felt an indescribable pull. Scarcely aware of what she was doing, she dropped the hoe and began to walk slowly toward the male, as if he were somehow pulling her with his mind. The closer she got, the more identifiable the sensation became until she realized it was not some strange malady that was affecting her.

She wanted him, desired him so fervently she could barely catch her breath. She paused when she was still several yards away from him, fighting the overwhelming need to touch him, to feel his hands on her, to feel him inside of her.

His face was taut with his own needs. For several moments, neither of them moved so much as a hair's breadth. Finally, almost as if he feared she would somehow break the spell and flee, he leapt at her, catching her tightly against him. Blackness crowded close in Kathryn's mind. She fought it, yielding to her need to touch him. He was hard and muscular all over. His skin beneath her palm felt satiny, not slickly smooth like her own, but more like the plush of velvet. Her desire mounted, spiraled completely out of control and she rubbed her cheek along his chest and neck, breathing in the scent that was making her wild with need.

With an almost guttural growl, he disentangled himself from her, pushed her slightly away from him. Kathryn protested, reaching for him again. Before she quite knew what was happening, he'd hoisted her over his shoulder. Turning, he headed for the jungle at a running trot.

Relief flooded her. He was going to find a place for them and he was going to do something about her needs.

She couldn't wait long, though. She felt like she was going to die if he didn't do something--quickly. She began stroking the flesh she could reach, his back, the top of his buttocks. He almost tripped when she slipped her hand beneath his loincloth to dig her fingers into his bare buttock.

When he regained his balance, he began running a little faster. Finally, they reached a stream. The banks were covered with a mossy, low growing vegetation. The man half dropped half lay her on the cushiony ground and sprawled on top of her. Kathryn fought him, trying to push him far enough away to remove the thin sarong she wore to cover her nakedness, unwilling to allow any barrier between them. He subsided, leaning away from her in frowning confusion. When she'd removed her sarong, she grabbed the edge of his loincloth, trying to pull it off without untying it when she couldn't find the tie quickly enough.

He helped her, discarding it to one side. Kathryn stared at his erect cock hungrily for several moments and grabbed it, stuffing it into her mouth and sucking on it greedily.

A jolt went through him at her action He was too stunned at first even to react, though his fingers curled in instinctive fear in her hair. Within moments, he began to shake. Kathryn caressed him harder and faster, urging him to come. Abruptly, he pulled his cock free of her mouth, shoved her back against the moss and mounted her, thrusting his cock deeply inside of her in one swift motion that dragged a groan of deep satisfaction from her. She countered his trust, digging her nails into his back to urge him to thrust harder and deeper. Abruptly her culmination caught her, dragging a scream of ecstatic delight from her. It seemed to echo endlessly through the jungle, altering in tone and pitch, sounding loud and then distant as if the sound were bouncing from tree to tree.

She was still reeling in the aftershocks when she felt his great body begin to shudder and spasm as he found his own release. He melted bonelessly against her as the tension flowed from him, struggling to catch his breath. Kathryn drifted lazily on a cloud of bliss, smiling to herself, unwilling even to consider moving--until she felt his cock swelling uncomfortably inside of her again.

Instantly aroused once more, she arched against him. To her surprise and consternation, he uttered a protest--not that she could understand anything he said, but the tone and timber of his voice was unmistakable. Puzzled, she went still. Apparently satisfied that she'd understood him, he eased slightly away from her. Holding her hips, he rolled onto his side to relieve her of his weight and began stroking her almost lovingly, murmuring soft words she knew instinctively must be a lover's praise. Enchanted, she lay perfectly still, listening to the musical sound of his voice.

A thrashing in the brush drew the attention of both of them. The male tensed. A moment later Kathryn felt the tightness in her passage recede and he withdrew from her.

Jumping to his feet, he surveyed the jungle around them carefully, his body tense, as if he was ready to spring into battle at the least sign of a threat. Finally, he relaxed and looked down at her, smiling faintly.

Kathryn smiled back, studying him now with curiosity. Beyond the sense that he was braced and ready to defend her, she saw nothing about him that was the least bit threatening. He was a beautiful creature. Except for his strange eyes and his odd flesh colorations, he might have been mistaken for a human.

He wasn't human. The loincloth indicated some advancement in civilization, but he undoubtedly hailed from a fairly primitive tribe of people.

He held out his hand to her and when she took it he helped her to her feet and very tenderly dressed her in her sarong once more. When he'd settled his loincloth on his hips, he lifted his head as if listening. After a moment, he called out, then listened again. A few moments later she heard a series of answering calls.

Apparently satisfied, he took her hand and began to lead her through the forest. Doubts surfaced, but Kathryn was far more curious than frightened. It might have been otherwise if not for the strange sensations that had swept over her when she'd first seen him. As it was, she was still more than a little disoriented by the expenditure of passion and she didn't even think to protest. They'd been walking for perhaps twenty minutes when they reached a clearing where nothing more than waist high vegetation grew. The man stopped there, as if waiting. Mentally shrugging, Kathryn waited, too, wondering what to expect. A few moments later a second male emerged from the jungle leading Maya, who followed him as docilely as she'd followed the male leading her. A second and third pair emerged shortly behind them. Within fifteen minutes Kathryn realized that everyone who'd been working in the fields with her had joined her, and the males, in the clearing.

They simply stared at each other in confusion for several moments. Slowly, it dawned upon Kathryn that the 'echo' she'd heard in the forest hadn't been an echo at all. There wasn't one woman who wasn't wearing a sappy, totally satisfied expression, despite the fact that several of them were beginning to look uneasy.

The male she was with laid a hand along her cheek. It was caressing in nature, not threatening and the look in his strange golden eyes was pure promise. He spoke to her, low, his tone gentle and finally released his hold on her. Uncertain of what he'd said, Kathryn merely stayed where she was for several moments. Finally, deciding he had no intention of objecting to her joining her friends, she moved toward the women, who had begun to form an uneasy knot in the center of the ring.

"What's going on, do you think?" Maya whispered.

Kathryn sighed. "I think I'm in love."

Maya snickered and slapped her hand playfully. "Be serious."

"I am serious," Kathryn said, grinning.

"You think we're in trouble?" Melinda asked a little nervously.

"Mmm, if that was trouble I'll have some more."

Melinda reddened. "Can you be serious?" she demanded.

Kathryn sighed. "Look, I've got no more idea of what's going on than the rest of you, but if you ask me, I think we've just been rescued."

* * * *

Da-vede found it difficult to take his eyes off of his new mate for fear she would simply vanish and he would discover it had all been no more than a wondrous dream. When he saw, though, that she seemed perfectly content to wait for him, he finally dragged his attention from her and glanced at his friend, Trinan. "What do you think?"

Trinan was trying hard to suppress the imbecilic grin that kept curling his lips. He shook his head. "We have searched so long I had become convinced that Ja-rael had lied to us and we would never find the village of the maned lions. I can not believe my good fortune! Is my mate not the most wondrous creature you have ever seen?"

Da-vede agree, although he had eyes for no other than his own mate and no clue of which one Trinan had laid claim to.

Trinan sobered after a moment, looking perplexed. "They are--not at all like our females. Did yours try to bash your head in with a stone when you had finished mating?"

"Yours did?" Da-vede asked in surprise. "Why would she do that?"

Trinan shrugged. "I do not know. I can not understand a word she speaks, but she seemed pleased with me--until we stopped."

"Perhaps that was it? She wasn't ready to stop."

"You think?" Trinan asked unhappily. "I will have to try harder to please her next time."

Da-vede nodded, but his thoughts were elsewhere. "There were not many males--and we have not paid a bride price."

Trinan turned to look at him. "You can not be considering going back to do so? Not when we made off with all the women? I'll admit I was--preoccupied at the time, but they were yelling and jumping up and down furiously as I ran into the woods. They are more likely to try to kill us than to negotiate a bride price."

Da-vede's lips tightened. "They can try--I don't like leaving without paying a bride price. My mate is more valuable to me than life. I do not wish to shame her by not paying."

"They might demand to have them back instead," Trinan pointed out. "And I, for one, will not give my mate up!"

Da-vede didn't like the sound of that. He didn't mind fighting for the right to take her if it came to that, but he would not give her up if they weren't satisfied with what he could offer. Finally, reluctantly, he decided that Trinan was right. "Let us move them to a safe place to stay the night. I will go with some of the others and leave the bride price at their village and then we will go home."

The End